IDENTITY

Chris Boult

Published by New Generation Publishing in 2017

Cover design photograph by Ryan Wood age 12

First Edition

www.newgeneration-publishing.com

New Generation Publishing

About the Author

Chris studied in Nottingham in the late 1970s. He joined the OTC and the TA and later served as a short-service officer in the regular army before joining the probation service in 1986. He served as a probation officer in various settings and at different levels, working mostly with high-risk offenders and often closely with both the police and the prison service. He retired from service in 2015. He started writing novels in 2013, and this is his fifth book.

Website: chrisbcultauthor.co.uk

Previous titles:

In The Shadow of the Bayonet

'The story is a good read, quite a page turner.'

'More interesting than the whodunit novels in this genre.'

'The book explores themes of justice, political intrigue and civil-military relations with an international dimension.'

Out of the Shadow

'Chris's rich and varied life experiences enable him to write pacey tales with a strong central character.'

'Another triumph, looking forward to the next book.'

'It was brilliant, had my emotions going, an excellent follow on.'

Recovery

'Excellent third book... Well written and particularly gripping.'

Acknowledgements

Thanks to all who continue to support me in this venture and take time to read my books and give me feedback. In particular, thanks to: my sister for help in proof reading, my publisher, Anglo Welsh Waterways at Great Haywood and Titanic Brewery for their assistance. Also to Ryan Wood who at age 12 has an incredible talent for photography and who kindly took the picture for the cover.

In honour of all those who toiled to build our canals.

'When I discover who I am, I'll be free.'

Ralph Ellison 1914–1994,
American author

Author's Note

In a world of high anxiety and constant change, old certainties no longer exist, leaving people asking ever more difficult questions about themselves and their background; their very identity. This is the theme of the book written through the eyes of a young probation officer – Rory Scott. I hope you enjoy it.

The story is set in the present time, in mid-Staffordshire with many of the places being real, although I have indulged in some poetic licence.

A look forward. .

There will be more books to come. I have started planning the next book; a different tale, back to my military routes, a compilation of history and stories from the Staffordshire Regiment. However more stories about Rory, Emma and Bracken could follow…

Glossary of terms

Banged up – imprisoned.

The Block – traditionally the punishment block for misbehaving prisoners, more recently referred to as the care and support unit.

Grassed them up – informed the authorities.

CPS – Crown Prosecution Service.

TSP – Thinking Skills Programme.

Mandatory life sentence – an automatic sentence for certain offences, principally murder.

Discretionary life sentence – a sentence awarded at the discretion of the Judge for other offences including manslaughter.

PART ONE

Chapter One

'Hi, Laura, it's Shaun, just to give you the heads up, there's another celebrity sex case about to hit the media; allegations have been made against Chas, the radio presenter, of abuse of young boys. His real name is Donald York, remember him?'

'Oh right, yes vaguely. Radio Mercia wasn't it?'

'Yes, that's right.'

'OK, well thank you for that. When is it likely to come to court?'

'Today, Laura, it's a very strong case against him that we've been investigating for some time. He was charged late last night with two initial counts of sexual assault of young boys supplied to him from Auldbeck, the old children's home, before your time probably. Apparently, he used to do publicity and fundraising for the home which was run by a voluntary Christian fellowship; in return they supplied regular access to children for him to abuse. Usually runaways, short-term stays, so often not missed and not followed up.'

'How, did it come to light then, Shaun?'

'Well, two of his victims later became journalists and met coincidentally at a press convention, and once they realised their connection and shared their experiences, eventually they decided that they were ready to approach the authorities and make statements. Their accounts were very thorough, detailed and quite plausible. It's a horrific level of abuse, Laura. I don't want to overload him but this one really will need an experienced officer from your side – it has Rory Scott written all over it.'

'Um, OK, I'll need to think about that; as you know, Rory's had more than his fair share of exposure to this kind of work recently.'

'OK, I'll leave it with you,' said Shaun putting down the phone and rushing off to a press conference before Donald York's first appearance in court that morning and an anticipated remand in custody. For Shaun, there was always that copper's sense of satisfaction to see a culprit behind bars and this case, of all the cases that he had dealt with recently, was crying out for precisely that.

Chapter Two

Rory Scott had always had a fascination with criminal justice and with people in general, with all their strengths and failings. That was what had driven him to want to work with people, to help give them opportunities and to enhance their lives. In time that was what led him to become a probation officer. Although still a young man, he now had four years' experience working in a community supervision team in Upper Lowbridge in mid-Staffordshire. He had already established himself as a capable and well-respected officer, with a particular interest in working with sex offenders. He looked forward to the opportunity at some point to perhaps work in Stafford Prison, a specialist establishment for sex offenders, and possibly helping in the programmes team delivering the sex offender treatment programme: SOTP. He supervised his cases diligently and wrote very insightful reports for the courts to aid them in the sentencing process. Rory was acutely aware of his social responsibility and of the harm done by sex offenders. He was committed to trying to work with them, but also realistic about the limitations and prepared to use the powers available to him in order to protect the public.

Rory's family background had no connection with criminal justice. His parents had been hard-working business people, who in some ways never really understood Rory's motivation for wanting to engage in this type of work. His father had always said to him that dealing with other people's troubles was a recipe for stress, anxiety and pressure, without reward, and that neither the public nor the punters would ever thank him for it. At times Rory totally rejected this analysis, but there were other darker times when he feared that maybe his father had been right.

He often wondered what draws people in a certain direction to want to work in a particular field? Rory always felt that he knew this was the area of work that he was meant to engage in. Much to his father's regret and condemnation he never felt drawn to work in business or finance. In the end, despite family pressure, he had chosen to go with his heart. His father had almost threatened to reject him when, at eighteen, he turned down a position in the family firm and opted to go travelling instead. His father was outraged by what he saw as disloyalty and a lack of appreciation for all that he had done for Rory. The very notion of 'a year out' was anathema to him for someone who hadn't even started his working life yet. Contrast that with his own experience of starting work at fifteen and working six or seven days a week ever since; a mantra that he often bestowed on Rory to the point of irritation.

That afternoon Rory was writing a fairly standard pre-sentence report for a drink-drive case, anticipating whatever he said that given a reading of 'three times over the limit' and the fact that this was a second offence in similar circumstances, that custody was inevitable. As he wrote the conclusion, offering a package of community supervision including unpaid work and attendance at a drink-drive programme, his mind started to drift off to his childhood. He'd often felt at odds with his family, particularly in not sharing his father's passion for making money...

The sudden ringing of his phone brought him back to the present; it was Laura, the team manager, asking him to come to her office. He liked her. Laura Mitchell was a popular team manager with a gift for communication, a strong work ethic and a good mind for process, statistics and policy.

As Rory got up he wondered what she wanted, but was happy to be taken away from the report that he had just about finished writing anyway.

'Yes, Laura, you wanted to speak to me,' he said as he entered her office at the end of a large open-plan area.

'Indeed. Yes come in, Rory, sit down,' she said, as she

4

moved papers off the nearest chair. 'I want to talk to you about a new case.'

'OK, whatever,' he replied nonchalantly, 'just put it through allocation as usual, I'll deal with it.'

'No, this one is different. I wanted to talk to you about it first. It's another sex offender case, and I know this is a field of professional interest for you, but I'm conscious of potentially overloading you. Have you the capacity for another case of this sort?' she asked with genuine concern.

'It's nice to be asked,' he replied, rather surprised, managers don't usually, he thought. 'Yes, I think so, what's it about and what makes it special?' he asked.

Laura started to explain how she had taken a call from Detective Chief Inspector Shaun Elder this morning and about the circumstances of this case.

'From the little I know so far, Rory, this is a case that will attract considerable public and media interest and could well result in a substantial sentence. I understand that the indications are that he intends to plead guilty. The evidence is overwhelming apparently. Further victims will no doubt emerge regarding the unsavoury arrangements he had with the leaders of the children's home.'

Rory didn't hesitate. He liked a challenge and was used to working hard with long hours. He had at least picked that up from his father.

'Yes, OK I can deal with that. I'll look forward to receiving the initial information from court and from the Crown Prosecution Service.'

Rory returned to his desk and opened an email from his sister inviting him to some corporate function that she knew he would hate. He always felt that she had sold her soul to a corporate giant but she seemed happy with it, much to the satisfaction of their father. It grated on him occasionally that even his own family, especially his own father didn't seem to know or understand him at all sometimes. He always felt a strong ambivalence towards his sister; he liked her very much but often wondered why?

'Are you alright, Rory, you look perplexed?' asked Joseph Oba, a kindly fellow officer. Joseph was of African origin with a calm, considerate disposition. Diversity in the team was important Rory felt, in order to be able to understand the mixed community they served. Joseph offered insight that often others didn't have. He had a sense of what life might have been like for young children caught up in conflict. He intrinsically understood how people might have to flee from their country, to have grown up without natural parents, or to be considered alien, to be foreign from a faraway land. Not to fit in, to be accepted or at times even wanted. To know rejection, even hate. No wonder first generation refugees sometimes drifted into crime or indeed were forced into it by unscrupulous criminal gangs who had seemed to offer hope, but who had only delivered purgatory. Joseph too had known suffering, but he had come through it and managed to hang onto to a faith and a love of humanity.

'You look troubled, my friend,' he commented. 'Can I help you?'

'Oh, Joseph, if only you could but thanks for asking anyway. How about a pint after work at The Stag and Fawn?'

'If you wish, of course, we can talk about it then!' he replied before easing away to meet the next offender who was waiting for his attention.

Chapter Three

It seemed strange to see his face after all these years. As a child Lee always remembered Chas, or Mr Chas as he used to refer to himself, as such a big man. Now he was old and grey, forlorn, strained, even haggard, not that of course that Lee felt in any way sorry for him, not after what he had put him through. From his position at the rear of the local court, Lee listened intently as the court went through its formalities; asking the defendant to confirm his name and address before putting the charges to him and announcing that, as expected, he would be remanded in custody. As Lee saw Mr Chas being led away by two burly escort staff to a waiting secure van, the irony of the proceedings invoked the beginnings of tears in his eyes. This wizened old man that he had just witnessed being taken away would only be likely to suffer a few relatively comfortable years in prison, opt out of being challenged about his offending and die well before the end of his sentence. Contrast this, Lee thought with the life sentence that the old bastard had left him with; constant fear, not being able to trust almost anyone, wondering why, wondering what possible pleasure could Mr Chas have taken from his obvious distress? Indeed his was a far worse fate than anything the courts could conceivably hand out to this thoroughly wicked man. Lee wondered whether he would ever truly trust anyone ever again, whether he would ever really feel comfortable with himself, whether he would ever even have a vision of what he might have been, rather than the drunken, insecure, lonely, single man that he evidently was.

* * *

It was times like these that took Lee back to the beginning, and the nagging thought that would it have been better if he too had been on that plane? He remembered the scene

7

so well and had played it back over and over in his mind many times. The holiday was booked, but he had contracted flu just before they were due to depart. His neighbour had offered to let him stay with them, his parents were grateful for the offer and carried on with their holiday plans. He remembered the disappointment of being told that he wasn't going with them, but the joy at the prospect of staying next door with his friend and his friend's Mum. If he had gone, he too would have been killed when the plane crashed and set his life on a path to self-destruction. He remembered the social worker with the blue coat coming to tell him that his parents were dead. He had no other family who could take him in. He remembered being taken away with just a small suitcase to a place with other children. Auldbeck; the very name made him shiver. He thought of the ghastly man who was charged with the care of these vulnerable children and how he so easily betrayed that trust and responsibility.

As he walked away from court, with mixed emotions, he passed the camera crew and the senior police officer describing how the public were being protected from Donald York. That despite budget cuts, his force would continue to prioritise investigations into historical sexual abuse. For the senior officer maybe this was success, Lee thought, but for him it just rekindled the torment.

As a child Lee Wilson had stayed at Auldbeck for just six months before being moved through a series of foster placements eventually to settle with an older couple of sisters who had offered him stability. He realised now that they weren't sisters at all of course, they must have been a gay couple, but nobody knew or spoke of such things back then. That was irrelevant now, and they had been kindly. After all the disruption to his education, Lee remembered the teacher at the local school who he had related to. The one who helped him discover his passion for reading and for books, the one who encouraged him and gave him some self-belief to apply to University. Swansea University had nurtured and rescued him. The experience had been liberating. Lee had gone into journalism with the local press and eventually, despite his battles with alcoholism, had progressed to being able to indulge his passion for writing book reviews for a larger regional newspaper.

As he continued to walk away from the court Lee knew that he needed to speak to Karl – Karl Gardener – who he had first met at Auldbeck.

Chapter Four

Rory returned home after another busy day. The office was always busy, there was no respite. His salvation was the peace and tranquillity of home. Rory was not in a position to afford to live entirely independently, so had rented a room with several others in an old house in the village of Millfield on the Shropshire Union Canal. Waiting for him at home as ever, was his dog Bracken – a Labrador, Springer and Staffy cross. Rory was offered the dog as a puppy from a local farm where he bought fresh vegetables from their farm shop and he was aware that their bitch was expecting a litter. They didn't want to keep all six puppies and were happy to give them away to anyone that they thought would look after them. When offered first choice of the bunch he jumped at the chance, eagerly selecting the first pup to come to him when he beckoned them. It was a light-brown colour like bracken, he thought, and the name stuck. They had quickly bonded and the dog turned out to be well behaved and responsive to his attempts to train him in at least the basics of walking to heel and obeying simple commands.

Rory set off to walk along the canal towpath with Bracken, as he often did. It was early spring and Rory liked the lighter evenings and the chance to sit outside, often at The Old Plough in the village for a pint. The pub was a free house and always kept a selection of local ales including Limestone, Slater's and Titanic. He walked along thinking of his new case and the work and challenges to come. How could someone in the public eye use that position to abuse children? Despite his theoretical knowledge and some real professional experience, the motivation for sexual offending still disturbed him. Maybe that was a good thing, he thought? *So Chas – Mr Chas – how many more victims are there still out there? How many more charges will result from further police investigation?* he wondered as he approached the pub, and

Bracken ran back to him with a dead pigeon in his mouth.

'Oh, Bracken, did you kill it?' he enquired, as if expecting the dog to answer.

His faithful dog looked up at him innocently. Looking at his prey it was evident that it had been dead for some time and would have been best left where he found it, but he suspected that Bracken would not agree. As Rory approached the pub garden his phone rang, it was his colleague Joseph from the office.

'Hi, Rory, sorry I missed you before you went, are you still up for that pint?'

'Yes, but I'm at The Old Plough now, not the Stag and Fawn.'

'OK, I'll join you there in about ten minutes.'

Rory was pleased at the prospect of some company. He tied Bracken to his usual metal ring by the water bowl for dogs and went into the pub. Captain Smith from Titanic was this week's guest local ale, so he ordered a pint. The beer was a sweet, strong and satisfying ale.

He returned to Bracken and sat on the bench overlooking fields and the countryside. It wasn't long before Joseph arrived and they unpicked the highlights of the cases of the day.

'So you've copped for that sex case again, Rory?' Joseph asked, seeking confirmation.

'Yes, it's going to be interesting!'

'No doubt. Are you sure you're OK with another case like this, I remember how the last one affected you.'

'Oh, in what way?'

'Come on, don't be such a hero! These cases touch your heart and your soul. There's something there, something that unnerves you, I can sense it.'

'I wouldn't be human if it didn't!'

'True, but just be careful and look after yourself. OK?'

'Yes, Dad,' Rory replied joking.

They talked about the team, the service, the manager before turning to the prospects for Stoke City this coming season and also for Port Vale, then Bracken barked reminding Rory it was time for his dinner. Before they headed for home, Rory returned to talking about work.

'Joseph, you know that other case of mine, the lad who doesn't know who he really is because his mother used to shag anyone so his father could have been any of them? Well, I saw him today and he was trying to explain how it is for him and I really felt I could understand, funny isn't it?'

'You think too much, I'll see you tomorrow.'

'Come on, Bracken, time for dinner!'

Chapter Five

'Karl, it's Lee.'

'OK, have you heard?'

'Yes, that's why I'm ringing, remanded in custody.'

'Yes and I hope he gets a good kicking,' replied Karl with feeling.

'Is that it now? Will he stay in there for ever?'

'Who knows. I only know that he deserves it. I wonder if anyone else will come forward now after all these years? There must be others, lots of them. I wonder where they are now?'

'Anywhere in the world, Lee, look what happened to me!'

Karl had been taken into care at birth in the 1960s. His poor mother was a young nurse who had become pregnant by the doctor she was seeing. She had been persuaded by family and social pressure to give up work, go into hiding, have the baby then give it up immediately for adoption. The doctor carried on unscathed and she never saw him again or of course her baby. Karl went initially to foster parents then to various children's homes, including Auldbeck until he was shipped out to Australia with countless other children as 'farm fodder' to help build the empire. Karl had been placed with a good family, others weren't so lucky, but as soon as he was eighteen he was rejected and knew that he wanted to return to England. He had managed to stay on another farm for a while to earn enough money to travel home and had returned to England in 1985 with nothing and no contacts. Re-establishing himself was tough but he did manage to complete his education whilst working in a variety of temporary and casual jobs. Eventually his interest and participation in sport gave him not only a stake in the local community but an opening with a local paper as a reporter and it was through that connection that the two men had met up again all those years later.

The process of deciding to expose Mr Chas and report him to the police was a painful one. They had met at a journalists' convention and recognised each other more from the delegates list than by appearance. The reunion had been difficult for them both, reopening old wounds, forcing reminders of events buried deep in their memories, events they wanted to remain there. Once they were brought back together, however, they both knew that could not happen and that they had a duty to report it; a duty to the other children and indeed more importantly to any children that he may still have contact with. They didn't know then but suspected that their treatment at the hands of Mr Chas had been similar. They were only to discover later the horrifyingly consistent pattern described by other victims.

When they did report it to the police they were well received and treated with sympathy and sensitivity. They were both considered to be reliable witnesses and their stories had triggered a wider investigation. Officers had uncovered some records of expressions of concern about the care provided at Auldbeck, but Donald York himself had not been directly implicated before.

The police had managed to trace some members of staff from that period. The home itself had been closed long ago. Two of those staff in particular were able to offer some collaboration of the men's account. They recalled being bemused why short-term children often seemed to be out of the home during the evenings and on return always seemed subdued, almost frozen. One of the male staff used to escort them, and no explanation for their absence was ever offered or given. One of them also remembered meetings between the home's manager, who was called the 'house parent' at the time and Chas, a prominent local character and radio presenter. Money seemed to flow into the home for extras; trips for the children, clothes, parties for staff and extra food for the kitchens. People didn't seem to make the connection between the two sets of events at the time. They just seemed to accept the situation and there was an internal culture not to ask too many questions.

Chapter Six

DCI Shaun Elder and Detective Sergeant Becky Jackson were reviewing the state of their investigation into the connections between Auldbeck and Donald York.

'So, let's summarise – what have we got so far?' stated Shaun, knowing that he would be required to present a summary to the Assistant Chief Constable at the afternoon regular meeting on progress with operation Uncover.

'Well, we seem pretty sure that York was paying off the home; after all this time we know that records are sketchy, but we have circumstantial evidence in the statements from the ex-workers there,' she replied.

'OK, we know the ACC will ask for more than that, so I want you to investigate bank accounts, old records of this voluntary organisation and similar records of York's financial affairs. His records will probably be the better source of information. We need to establish a verified link if we are going to be able to investigate the involvement of others.'

'OK, Boss. We've established that Gerald Ross, the House Manager at the time at Auldbeck is still alive. He's now in his nineties and living in a care home in Sussex.'

'Um, yes we may have some difficulty convincing the CPS that it's in the public interest to pursue a man in his nineties. However, they do seem more willing to pursue cases regardless of age, these days.'

'Surely, Sir, the principle is if a crime has been committed then it's been committed?'

'Yes, but politics gets in the way and the fact that there have been a series of these cases that have fallen with much embarrassment, not to mention cost, doesn't help. Anyway, that's not a decision for us. I'm with you, I'd still like to nail him.'

'Have any more people come forward claiming to have been victims from the past, Sir?'

'Yes, we have three cases currently being investigated

in other areas of the country.'

'Well that's promising then!'

'Yes, I'll catch you later at the meeting. Let's hope the ACC is in an incisive mood and we're not there too long!'

* * *

'Right, folks, let's get started,' announced Assistant Chief Constable David Glyn, as the assembled group shuffled papers and took deep breaths. The ACC in this instance was old school, with a long service record although he was coming towards the end of his time. Not too soon some thought, but he did bring experience and a long memory, which in such historical cases had its advantages.

'That's everyone today, Sir. I have reports from the two other officers not present.'

'OK, Shaun, let's have your summary.'

'Sir, the good news is that Donald York was remanded in custody this morning and the CPS are sounding confident of a conviction and a substantial sentence, effectively meaning that he is never likely to be released. Investigations into the financial irregularities are ongoing and I have tasked Sergeant Jackson this morning to concentrate more on that aspect. Reports are awaited from the three other forces currently investigating allegations from ex-residents, but indications are solid that their stories are tangible and that further charges will follow. Should the other forces follow through with that, Sir, then the eventual sentence will reinforce what I've already said so there isn't much mileage in pursuing any other ex-residents.'

'I disagree on that point, Shaun. We must remember that this is about uncovering the truth, and although it may not result in any further lengthening of what will undoubtedly be a long sentence, it is still important to the victims to be heard,' replied the ACC, reinforcing his authority.

'Yes of course, Sir.'

17

'So I want you to be more proactive in trying to establish a wider picture. Chasing old records of residents' names and being more systematic in trying to trace them, rather than waiting for them to come to you, for example.'

'I see, Sir.'

The meeting continued for another thirty minutes on minor procedural details and then broke up leaving the team to carry on. Shaun walked back to the office with Becky.

'I wish he hadn't said that; now we have to start trailing through what could be hundreds of names of ex-residents who could be anywhere in the country, if not the world! Oh well, he's the ACC.'

Chapter Seven

Rory was starting to go through the CPS and court papers in the York case. The content and the implications were stark, those poor children, he thought. Already frightened and confused by their sudden arrival in care, the victims were taken to a place York used, strangely enough it seemed, the same place on every occasion. A small cottage he owned in the country, miles from anywhere with no neighbours. They would be dropped off by the same man, one of York's staff who apparently was well paid for the service, and then systematically abused. Abuse included indecent or sexual assault; the term had changed in law over the intervening time, including having acts forced on them and them being forced to perform acts on York. No one else was ever involved in the assaults and no one ever alleged that it went as far as rape, but nevertheless it must have been horrific. Victims consistently reported crying, screaming, shouting, even biting in an attempt to get away but he was always too strong.

After their ordeal they would be threatened and sworn to secrecy and then collected by the same man and taken back to the home. Other staff must have known, surely, Rory thought, but only two were prepared to testify. In both cases they reported seeing children identified, usually young, both sexes and taken by this man. No one dared question it at the time such was the grip York had on his staff and no one talked about it afterwards. The victims were then usually moved on quickly to other homes or placements, often, according to the victims for further abuse. Records were minimal, accountability was non-existent and no enquiries were ever entered into. Incredible! This was not a case of abuse by the powerful or the authorities knowing or suspecting and choosing to ignore it, or actively covering it up, this was actually not reported at all. It was as if these poor children did not exist, no one cared, they were not important, just social unfortunates, casualties that the state was grateful to hand over to 'worthy' charitable organisations with no questions asked – and this was only fifty-odd years ago! Rory felt himself beginning to get upset and moved away from his desk, taking solace in the kitchen. It was time for a coffee.

Yuan, another officer joined him for her morning Chinese tea.

'OK, Rory? You look shocked.'

'That's because I am. I've just read the York papers; they are horrific!'

'Oh dear, I understand. You must share it with us, Rory – the burden I mean. Don't take it all on yourself; release the negative feelings, they can be powerful and destructive.'

He thanked her, as he knew she was right. Yuan Lin was a fine young officer, one who again brought something different, something unique to the team. She was very bright, spoke six languages and was an absolute wiz with computers.

Rory smiled as he passed Sophie Cooper at her desk, the fourth officer in the team. Sophie was a little older and probably wiser, quite motherly, warm and empathic. She had a special interest in supporting women who had been subjected to domestic violence, and she was also good at dealing with the men who were responsible. She was very firm about boundaries and behaviour and most offenders responded to that.

Rory was concerned about the failure to comply by the young man he had mentioned to Joseph. Kasman Jones was on licence, having been released from prison for drugs offences. He was an angry and bitter young man, not without cause but using and selling drugs wasn't helping anybody as a coping strategy. Rory was often amused and bemused at the names offenders seemed to acquire from parents who he supposed were trying to be helpful, responsible or original – who knows? Kasman had often spoken to him about his feeling that his mother couldn't actually tell or remember who his father was, so he had never met him, not knowingly at least. Kasman hadn't had a relationship with his mother for years either – she was found dead on waste ground near where they lived, when he was only a child. Her sister had taken him in, but she was no more reliable and eventually kicked him out at fifteen when she caught him having sex with the girl next door in the garden shed, when both of them should have been in school. Rejected and expelled, Kasman lied about his age and tried to join the army but failed to get through the training. The rigour and the discipline were too much for him and he was discharged after a fight with one of his instructors. After that he returned to working on the travelling fair, living rough, having casual sex and taking too many drugs.

As Kasman was not responding to the conditions of his licence, he faced being sent back to prison. Rory was not in favour of the automatic use of this procedure, known as breach, at the first suggestion of a hiccup; he preferred to persevere but the system was against him. He knew that at this stage he would have no discretion, no choice but to instigate breach proceeding against Kasman. He knew that he would be arrested as soon as the police could find him and returned to prison to serve out the remainder of his five-year sentence. In some ways custody could be a sanctuary for the likes of Kasman with the prospect of drying out and stabilising, but it was a harsh and crude approach to rehabilitation. Equally, given the concerns about the ready availability of drugs in prison, it could even make his addiction worse. Rory feared that for Kasman the wounds were too deep, too entrenched to realistically be able to recover and that the prognosis for his survival outside of the system was poor.

By the afternoon when Kasman had not responded to a morning appointment, Rory processed his breach application. It was not an emergency, but usually offenders in these circumstances were picked up within a couple of days unless they were deliberately trying to evade arrest. For Kasman, as he suspected the reality of what day it was had alluded him and he was sitting in a rundown B&B having also missed his appointment with the job centre. He wasn't even conscious of his inactions and frankly was past caring. He hated the world and most of all he hated himself, whoever he was.

Rory was due to see Laura for supervision before the end of the working day. Supervision, an old concept originally envisaged more for staff support, had become all about accountability. Laura checked his performance against her spreadsheet looking for any amber or red indicators. She quizzed him about progress with his high-risk cases and his compliance with his annual appraisal objectives. She was thorough and very efficient. Finally, she turned to him and asked if he had anything to discuss?

Rory cleared his throat and really just wanted to get out of the office but had already decided to raise the single most pressing issue for him; that of his own identity. His current cases had only served to remind him of his own torment about who he really was. He had always felt ill at ease with his parents and family. He liked his sister although they were very different in character and appearance, but he just didn't relate to his parents. He had 'escaped' at the first opportunity from their world of materialism, high performance, high expectations and little tolerance for those who were unable to compete or chose not to join them.

Laura listened as she had been trained to do and nodded, giving him space to express his feeling. Then glancing at her watch remarked, 'Look, Rory, it's not unusual for probation officers to have strong feelings and reactions when dealing with offenders. We're human too and we deal with humanity in the raw. I'm afraid it goes with the territory. In many ways it's what makes the job attractive, but at times it can be more than challenging. If you feel that you need to deal with this separately, outside supervision, then I can only commend the staff counselling service to you. Many of us use it and find it helpful, perhaps it's time for you to explore this issue more thoroughly?'

As Rory walked away he thought that maybe she was right, she often was.

Chapter Eight

Becky Jackson was diligently following up her action from her DCI. She wasn't really getting anywhere with chasing old records from Auldbeck. The home had closed in the 1970s after a fire. Circumstances were suspicious; although nothing was ever proved, it did appear from police records at the time that such a catastrophic destruction of evidence could well have been more than convenient. The charity no longer existed and she rapidly concluded that she was unlikely to uncover any useful detail. Witness statements could be all that they had, unless she thought the tax authorities or Companies House may still have some files. She reminded herself of the need to be persistent and decided to proceed with that line of enquiry.

When she contacted the arrest team who had lifted York from his dingy flat she was pleased to hear that they had cleared, catalogued and stored its complete contents. There might be something incriminating there, she thought! Although it may well take days to sift through and find it, she would need authority for that, she concluded.

Meanwhile her DCI was speaking to his counterpart in Yorkshire about one of the other three victims who had come forward. His account was more harrowing and far more serious. The man in question claimed that both he and his younger sister had been sent to Auldbeck after being taken into care in 1972 when their parents were both killed in a train crash. He was adamant that both he and his sister were taken to York's cottage together but that only he was brought back. He still remembers her screaming as he was dragged into the car and taken back to the home. He was moved on the next day and had never seen or heard from her since. He was convinced that York must have killed her.

Shaun thanked the officer and immediately ordered a

search of the house and grounds at the cottage. If the man was right then it was a high probability in his judgement that the body would be on that site.

Shaun then contacted HMP Downgate, the private prison where York was being held on remand. He wanted to know whether York had said anything that might help their enquiries. He was informed that no, York had said nothing that could be useful to the police and had totally refused to cooperate with any intervention from the prison. He had opted for vulnerable prisoner status to protect him from the other prisoners, many of whom would have had experience of the care system and would welcome the chance of retribution against one of its managers or associates. They also of course took a dim view of sex offenders in general and child sex offenders in particular. There certainly would be some prisoners who had been victims of sexual abuse themselves, or knew someone that had and would also want to tear him apart. Custody staff generally felt mixed loyalties about this dilemma; being charged with protecting a monster did not sit easily with many officers. There were times when they were tempted to turn him over to the other prisoners but thought better of it.

Before he rang off, Shaun had arranged to meet the designated police liaison officer covering Downgate and to interview York tomorrow about the grim disclosure of a possible murder. The young girl's name was Molly Bennett. There had never been a missing person's enquiry, simply because no one had reported her missing. Her brother wasn't in a position to do so and her family, such as they were, could have reasonably assumed that the state was taking care of the children.

Chapter Nine

Rory had been thinking about what Laura had said to him. He decided that he did want to refer himself to counselling. He had canvassed the opinion of others who had used the service, as she had suggested, and concluded that it could be worthwhile.

It was late in the evening and Rory was still sitting at his computer at home. At least with his job he reflected that you couldn't routinely bring official information home and work on it anymore, there had been too many security breaches, but he was just outlining some ideas in a Word document about a presentation that he had been asked to give to magistrates. Seeing the light still on in his room, one of his housemates had gently knocked at the door and walked in to check that he was OK.

'You alright, mate?' he enquired. 'It's late and I know you're an early riser.'

'Yes, it's kind of you to ask. I'll call it a day now,' he replied, genuinely appreciating the concern. He was lucky, he reflected, to have such good housemates who helped each other. There was an absence of the kind of conflicts and tensions that he often heard about in other similar circumstances. The little things that often niggle in shared living situations were normally dealt with without drama and with humour, which usually helped.

The house group complemented each other nicely in terms of their skills and interests. Some were good cooks or computer experts, whilst others were happy to keep the place tidy or do the garden and most of the residents were only too keen to take Bracken for a walk when required. In fact, he often had several walks in a day with various combinations of residents, which everyone seemed to enjoy.

Before turning in, Rory considered what he wanted to get out of counselling and determined to make contact with the service at work tomorrow. He hoped that it would be a chance to express and offload some of his negative feelings about his unease and misgivings, and what to do next. There you are, he thought, that's a simple and sound objective to start with!

Chapter Ten

Shaun presented his ID card at the prison gate, went through the comprehensive search procedure and proceeded into the prison visits room. There he met Sergeant Max Abeli. They talked and exchanged information while they waited for the prisoner to arrive.

'So how's the family, Max?'

'Good thanks, the girls are all doing well, the youngest has just joined the force!'

'That's great, Max, you must be so proud.'

'Oh yes and Maria is too.'

'Your prisoner is ready for you, gentlemen – we'll bring him in, interview room three.'

'Thank you. That's good, Max, you can wait for hours here sometimes!'

The two officers sat down, not perturbed by their forthcoming encounter, but realistically not expecting to get very far either.

'Mr York, sit down. I'm Detective Chief Inspector Elder and this is Detective Sergeant Abeli from Staffordshire Police, we are here to interview you about the disappearance of Molly Bennett who was at Auldbeck in 1972.'

'I've admitted responsibility for the current offences but do you seriously expect me to remember every child I met from Auldbeck over forty years ago?'

'Oh I think you'd remember this one, Mr York, you see she never came back, at least according to her brother.'

York recoiled visibly and shuffled uneasily in his plastic chair.

'The name means nothing to me.'

'No, you weren't interested in their names were you, Mr York, their identity was irrelevant to you, you just wanted to use them, but did you go too far with this particular young girl?'

York became more uncomfortable. 'What do you mean

exactly, what are you saying?' he asked, starting to become emotional.

'Mr York, it is alleged that her brother was taken back to the home leaving Molly with you screaming. What happened that night, Mr York?' enquired the DCI leaning forward and staring directly into his eyes.

'Oh yes that one,' he said starting to cry, 'she became hysterical, I didn't mean to harm her you understand!'

'But you had already sexually assaulted her, hadn't you?'

'Yes, er, maybe, I don't remember…'

'I think you do, Mr York. Did you kill her? Did you kill Molly Bennett that night in your cottage, Mr York, did you?'

Sobbing, York slumped in his chair. 'It's my biggest regret, I honestly didn't think that I was harming the children at the time, but she struggled, became inconsolable, hysterical and then she spluttered, coughed and started to struggle for breath. The more I tried to help, the more she panicked. I couldn't save her, she died in my arms. I didn't kill her, Chief Inspector. Honestly I didn't!'

Sensing a breakthrough Shaun continued, 'Did you call an ambulance, did you report it afterwards? No, where did you hide the body, Mr York? We need to know, her brother needs to know. Where is she, Mr York?'

Donald York got up to leave, 'I can't remember, Chief Inspector, I can't, I can't…'

A prison custody officer entered the room, having heard the disturbance.

'That's it, calm down, York. I'll have to take you back to your cell now. I'm sorry, gentlemen, but you've run out of time. I need to get him back for roll-call now, he's already late.'

'OK, Officer, we understand,' Shaun responded before turning to York: 'We'll find her, York, if she's there we'll find her.'

Spluttering, Donald York was led away back to his new life in custody.

'What did you make of that, Max?'

'He did it, Gov, I'd put money on it. She'll be buried in the garden.'

'Yes, you're probably right. I'll check with Yorkshire whether her brother remembers if she had any breathing difficulties.'

Chapter Eleven

Rory was feeling pleased with himself as he concluded his final session with an offender who had made real progress. Josh had been going through a rough patch after he was made redundant and debt had got on top of him. He had fallen for what seemed like the easy option at the time in order to keep his family going and had accepted a loan from a less than official source. The subsequent exorbitant interest payments only exacerbated his troubles and compounded his debt. When temptation presented itself in the form of theft, he had succumbed and got caught. Rory had worked with him for two years on supervision during which time Josh had been prepared to look at his decision making and problem solving processes and, with skills learnt on the Thinking Skills Programme, had really applied his learning well. He completed his unpaid work as part of the court order and secured a new job on better conditions and higher pay than he had before. This had enabled him to repay his debts, free himself from the loan shark and start to move forward.

Josh was also pleased with his progress and was grateful for the support that he had received and also felt that it had probably saved his marriage. As they parted for the final time, with the customary wish not to meet again, at least not in these circumstances, Rory felt reinvigorated. This was what he did the job for. Every once in a while despite all the frustrations and disappointments inherent in working with offenders, he would deal with a case that gave him real satisfaction. This was such a case and it came at just the right time to lift his spirits.

Yuan passed his desk later as he was finishing writing up the records and commented, 'You must have done a good job with that chap, Rory. I've not seen such a broad smile on leaving the office like that for a long time!'

'Thanks, Yuan. Yes sometimes it just clicks!'

'Good, take heart,' she replied, knowing that he had

been struggling of late.

As he finished his records his phone rang, it was Emma, his sister.

'Hi, Emma, how are you?'

'I'm fine, Rory, busy. Hey, I've had a meeting cancelled in Stoke today and just thought I could spend the evening with you, if you like?'

'Perfect!' he replied. 'What a good start to the weekend.'

'OK, how about meeting in Stone, we could have a drink in The Swan and eat at Granville's – shall I book it?'

'Yes do. See you in The Swan at six then.'

'OK,' and she rang off.

Rory helped Joseph complete a report he was writing that was required for Monday, before leaving the office early at four-thirty to go home and get changed in time to meet Emma at six. It was a comfortable drive from the office in Upper Lowbridge to his house in Millfield. Bracken was pleased to see him and had already had his walk with one of Rory's housemates. Generally, whoever went for a walk would take him with them, usually for his familiar run alongside the canal.

Rory showered and changed and one of his housemates drove him into Stone in time to walk into The Swan at five to six to find Emma sitting at a table, already waiting for him. She had got the first round in, what a girl! They greeted each other warmly as Rory pecked her on the cheek. He felt that he wanted more, but held back. What a good looking woman she was now, he thought. They talked enthusiastically about what was happening in their lives, their achievements, hopes and aspirations.

'Is there anybody in your life at the moment then, Sis?' he asked her.

'No, men try it on, but I'm too busy for all that, Rory.'

Emma had established herself in business, owned a flash car and an upmarket penthouse flat in Birmingham as a base, although she often travelled all over the country and abroad. Their parents owned a flat in London, overlooking the Thames and she often stayed there too. Short breaks in the family villa in Spain were also a bonus.

'So, how is my little brother these days then, still saving the world?' she enquired.

'You cynic. I'm OK. I've had a good day today.'

'You haven't sounded so good lately when I've caught you on the phone.'

'No, sometimes I get down, don't we all?'

'I suppose so. You always were quite serious, not like me at all. So what's been bothering you?'

'I suppose I just still feel confused sometimes, about who I am, what's it all about and where am I going?'

'Oh, just that. Nothing major then!'

They laughed and smiled at each other.

'You always had a thing about all that stuff. I don't even think about it.'

'You're lucky.'

'You can choose not to, you know. You've finished your drink, another pint? Shall I choose?'

'Yes please, do.'

Rory admired his sister for her matter-of-fact attitude as she confidently got up to walk to the bar past some admiring glances. She returned with her gin and tonic and his pint of the one of many real ales, the one with the most bizarre name.

'What's this one?' he enquired. 'Tastes nice though.'

'You shouldn't take things too seriously you know, we are young and unattached, why worry? You always felt that you didn't fit in and obviously didn't want to follow mum and dad's lifestyle, despite father's obvious irritation. So what? Just be your own man, Rory.'

The simplicity and directness of her advice really struck him. After a pause he changed the subject. They chatted and had another drink before heading off up Stone High Street to Granville's. Emma had booked for seven-thirty and it was very busy as usual. Granville's was special for both of them. It was where they grew up, where they had romanced with their friends and partied. The menu was good and they enjoyed their meal, relaxed, danced to the accompanying band and left feeling good. Rory had already mentioned that one of his housemates was away for the weekend and that Emma could have her room. Bracken would be pleased to see her again.

Emma was happy to pay for a taxi, so they set off to Millfield.

The following day they decided to drive up to The Staffordshire Moorlands with Bracken and walk around Biddulph Gardens, owned by The National Trust.

They drove through Stone to check that Emma's car was OK, then on up the A34 through Newcastle to Biddulph. They enjoyed a coffee in the little National Trust Shop before wandering around the gardens, with Bracken chasing anything that moved once they had entered the area where dogs were free to be off the lead.

'I wish I was more relaxed like you, Emma,' Rory commented.

'Well just try to be!' she replied. 'You really must put this parent thing to bed, Rory. There is no natural law that says we all have to be like our parents. Time moves on, each generation does things differently. There is no reason why you should automatically do as they did, why should you?'

'Yes but you have.'

'OK, but only because I choose to, not because I feel forced to, or that because it's expected.'

They walked on uphill through the impressive avenue of tall trees with the sun breaking through to warm the ground and provide patterns of light and shade. Rory became more relaxed in her company, it felt natural together. He almost wanted to hold her hand, but that would have been silly.

Emma told him how their mum and dad had been when she saw them last week, how they had asked after him. She described a business deal that she was working on, and although Rory was sure that this was not for him he was pleased by the obvious pleasure and satisfaction that

Emma drew from her work.

They drove back through Newcastle, stopping at McDonald's on the way for lunch before returning to Emma's car parked up in Stone by the police station for a sense of security. Emma had to rush off, but they parted having really enjoyed each other's company, catching up and sharing thoughts. Rory drew strength from their time together and almost felt renewed.

Returning to work on Monday, Rory was immediately under pressure to focus and put to one side his issues about his personal life. The contrast was stark but functional. Rory was on office duty and anticipated the usual queue of the desperate and the needy. Before he got very far in addressing his backlog of emails, reception asked him to respond to a someone who'd called in and was getting extremely agitated in the waiting room. He said that he had missed an appointment and was desperate to avoid being breached and sent back to prison.

Rory responded and came to meet him quickly, hoping to intervene before the situation deteriorated any further.

'Brian Farmer? Hi, I'm Rory, the duty officer today. Come on, let's have a chat about your situation and see if we can sort something out,' said Rory kindly but firmly.

'Rory, please don't breach me, mate, I really don't need to go back to prison, not now, not again… please understand me!' he replied, becoming emotional.

'Come in,' said Rory leading him into an interview room. 'OK, first tell me what happened.'

'Well, I got in the wrong company and ended up being part of a Post Office robbery,' said Brian in great haste. 'I got five years and have just got out on licence but I missed yesterday's appointment with the Chinese lady. Don't breach me please. I've just got a job. That's where I was yesterday, honest.'

'OK, Brian, calm down this may be retrievable. Is this your first missed appointment?'

'Yes, or no … well I'm not sure. I came in the afternoon instead of the morning once. Does that count?'

Rory was able to reassure him while confirming the clear and strict expectations about meeting his appointments whilst on licence. This is to reassure the public that community supervision means business, he explained, and it helps you get in the right frame of mind to run your life and make better decisions. 'Now tell me about this job?'

'Yes it's with a mate. He strips cars and sells the parts. He says that I can drive the van and help him in the workshop. Only a few hours mind and no guarantees but he reckons I'll do alright. That's good isn't it, Rory?'

Rory's heart sank. 'Have you got a driving licence, Brian?'

'Well, no, but I've been driving since I was a kid. I'm a good driver,' Brian insisted.

'Yes but no licence will mean no insurance and that's not safe is it, Brian? And that's two offences already.' Rory paused for the message to sink in. 'Brian, these cars that your mate strips, have you thought where they might come from?'

'Oh they're all from round here, Rory,' responded Brian confidently.

'No I mean were they cars bought and sold with the owner's consent, Brian?'

'I don't know, what do you mean?'

'Brian, come on think. You must have done the thinking skills programme in prison? This is a good chance to use those skills. You implied that you felt led astray in being drawn into the robbery offence and now you're telling me that you have got a job with a mate who strips down cars. Has it not occurred to you that those cars might be stolen, Brian, and that you are about to make the same mistake again?'

Brian looked stunned as the realisation dawned. 'Oh shit, Rory, I never thought of that,' he acknowledged. 'He's a mate.'

'Is he really, Brian, or is he just looking for a sucker to do his dirty work?'

Rory managed to talk to Yuan Lin to clarify Brian's position to avoid the breach that Brian feared most. They left him in no doubt that he had to turn down the job and look for something legitimate and reliable and that this was his last chance.

Chapter Twelve

Shaun rang his colleague in Yorkshire.

'Hi, it's Shaun from Staffordshire. We've interviewed York about Molly's death. He claims it was an accident. Can you ask her brother if he remembers if Molly had any breathing difficulties? It might be relevant.'

'OK, mate. Will do.'

Shaun had endorsed his sergeant's plan to trawl through the file retrieved from York's house in search of any financial information. Becky was due to start looking that day.

The file store was like some mega Argos warehouse as Becky walked down the neatly labelled rows to find the section she was looking for. Where to start? She pulled down several boxes which seemed to contain ornaments and pictures before finding two boxes containing various papers. She started to separate them into piles. After a while she found a couple of letters on headed paper. Barclays Bank. So at least she had found which bank he used. There were no statements, but some letters referring to investments of quite large sums. Not the sort of money you would expect someone working in his position to earn. Was that enough? She wasn't sure and felt that it needed to be referred to the financial crime specialists. Maybe they could access his bank records from Barclays with this new information? She left to report back.

When she returned Shaun was about to leave to join the search team at the cottage; bones had been found in the back garden and the pathologist was on site. As Becky started to describe what she had found, the phone rang.

'DCI Elder.'

'Mate, I've spoken to Molly's brother and yes he remembers clearly that she was severely asthmatic. He said she was just four years old when he lost her, by the way.'

'Thank you. I'll come back to you when I have a clear

picture to tell her brother. We have found bones in the back garden but it's not confirmed whether they are human yet, let alone been identified.'

He turned to Becky and said, 'OK, I'd better go. Tell me about your findings later, but follow it up, trust your judgement.'

'OK, Sir.' Right consult the financial crimes unit then, she thought.

As Shaun arrived at the cottage, a large number of official vehicles had gathered. Police cordon tape was in place and a tent erected around the find. He felt confident that Max was right, at least about Molly being in the garden. How she died may not be so clear, or easy to prove, he thought. As he walked through the groups of staff, ID card in hand, Shaun steadied himself for what was to come. It didn't get any easier, he thought, at least this body was likely to be no more than a skeleton, so not as shocking as a recent death.

He entered the tent where the pathologist was working. Uncovered was a full skeleton in good condition that looked human and was the size of a small child.

'DCI Elder,' he said crisply, 'So what have we got, doctor?'

'Well, it's human alright. Tests will need to confirm it, but in my judgement the skeleton is female.'

'Her brother tells us that Molly was four years old when she disappeared,' Shaun replied.

'Well then, this skeleton is consistent with Molly's age at the time,' responded the doctor.

'Any thoughts on cause of death?'

'As you know it's early days, but what I can say is that there is some slight misalignment of the neck bones, which would be consistent with strangulation, but don't quote me.'

'OK. Thank you. Anything else?'

'No, not at this stage. I'll have the report with you as soon as possible.' he replied helpfully.

All in a day's work, Shaun thought as he moved on to

speak to the search team.

'OK, folks? Anything useful to report, apart from finding the body?'

'No, Boss, nothing more yet, we'll check the whole garden and the house while we're here just in case there are others.'

'Yes please. I have nothing to suggest that there may be, but let's be sure before you go.'

Shaun got back in his car thinking of his own children as he often did at times like this. Poor kid, abandoned, abused and probably murdered at four years old. Shaun did not feel optimistic that he would be able to prove anything. Time had passed, York was the only witness and he claimed it was an accident, and it could be very hard to positively identify the body. It would probably be down to dental records. Before he left, Shaun returned to the scene to speak to the doctor again.

'Doctor, if you are right and she was strangled, would someone with severe asthma be more vulnerable in those circumstances?'

'Yes of course. If she was asthmatic she could have died with little or no intervention from him.'

'That's what I feared.'

'We have to let the evidence lead the way, Chief Inspector,' she responded calmly.

'Indeed. Will dental records be able to identify her?' Shaun asked.

'Possibly, but we'll be lucky.'

Before he drove away, Shaun rang Yorkshire again, 'Hi, it's me again, Shaun. Can you ask the brother if there are any dental records?'

'It's her then?'

'Probably, but it's not confirmed yet. You can tell him that we have found a body, female, about the age that Molly was when she went missing, that's all at this stage.'

'OK. I'll get back to you as quickly as I can.'

* * *

Becky was waiting for him when he got back. The cottage wasn't far out of Upper Lowbridge. They quickly exchanged information, pleased that they would have something tangible to the report to the ACC's round-up later.

'So, let's hope the finance team can extract some more information. That could draw others into the investigation. I'm waiting now for any news about dental history. Well done, Becky, that's good work.' They sat down to review some other cases, but it wasn't long before the phone rang.

'Shaun, it's me, the brother says there are no dental records. He said the likes of them never saw a dentist, she wouldn't even have been registered.'

'OK, thanks, that's a pity.'

The ACC were pleased with their efforts and the meeting ended with a sense of hope that they were getting somewhere. Momentum was so important in an investigation like this, Shaun thought as he left for home.

Chapter Thirteen

Rory kept thinking of what his sister had said and the common sense of her straightforward advice. He felt happy with that, just be your own man she had said. He liked that as a phrase, he could remember it and repeat to himself. He thought that he must mention that to the counsellor.

He was on office duty again today and was getting prepared for the usual onslaught of offenders reporting in, some OK, many in crisis; homeless, in debt, drunk, withdrawing from drugs. All would be featured today, no doubt. If he had the chance he would finish another court report in between seeing people as reception staff tried their best to filter out unnecessary interviews or time wasters. Laura wasn't in today either, so he was covering for her too. Too many hats, he thought? Yes of course, too much to do and never enough people to do it. He knew it had got worse even in his relatively short period of service, and if the proposed cuts were followed through it could only result in further deterioration. It was difficult to maintain morale in these circumstances, but he tried to stay positive. There is no merit in misery, an old university tutor used to say.

His phone rang; it was reception asking for his help to see a troubled young woman in interview room three. He didn't know the case. Her officer was in court today so he had a quick trawl of the file. Tracy O'Marney; benefit fraud, previous prostitution, some custody, history of domestic violence, some child care concerns – OK, fairly standard then, he thought as he got up to go and see her, notebook and pen in hand.

Rory introduced himself as he entered the room and sat down.

'Hello, Tracy, my name's Rory Scott. I'm one of the probation officers here. I'm sorry your own officer isn't available. I see you aren't due in today, so what brings you in, how can I help?'

As Tracy started to reply, she began to cry.

'Mr Scott, I'm in trouble again. I had a bad day yesterday and was on the gin so I've spent all the money for this week and it's only Monday. My fella will be back out of prison tomorrow and he'll knock the life out of me if there's no money. I don't want to have to sell myself again tonight but don't feel I have any choice,' she said as she sobbed.

'If the Social find out they'll take my kid away again and I don't think I'll get him back this time. That will be another beating. I might as well just run away or top myself.'

The phone rang – it was reception asking him to take an urgent call from Sophie Cooper. He was waiting for confirmation whether he would need to attend a brief meeting on Laura's behalf, which wouldn't be brief and he was all too aware that he wasn't going to be able to help Tracy all in five minutes. Which first? He thought he'd better take the call.

'I'm sorry, excuse me, Tracy, but I must just take this call,' he said, as he passed her a tissue. 'OK, put it through… Sophie, it's Rory, can I help?'

'Rory, I'm sorry I know staff numbers are tight today but my car's just broken down returning from my prison visit. The AA are here and say they'll need to tow me to a garage, the head gasket has gone apparently.'

'OK, best get it sorted, that won't be quick. Where are you exactly? Can you get back to the office alright?'

'I'd just come off the M5 to avoid congestion; they're suggesting taking me to Redditch, so I suppose it will be a taxi to the station and get a train back to Upper Lowbridge from there, I've no idea how long that will take!'

'OK, but you are alright?'

'Yes fine, it's just another expense I could do without. One thing, Rory, quickly, they are ready to go – my report for Crown Court tomorrow, the lady is coming in this afternoon for me to go through it, can you see her for me…' the signal broke and Rory replaced the phone.

'Tracy – right, here's a tenner,' he said reaching into his pocket and handing her a ten pound note. 'Don't spend it on booze, Tracy, it's for food for your kid. I'll give you a note to take to the local food bank to stock up your cupboards. I'll leave a note for your partner's officer to make sure he knows your circumstances and give a strict warning NOT to react with violence. If there is risk of trouble you must ring your emergency number to the police domestic violence unit – OK?'

'Yes, Mr Scott, I will. Thank you, Sir. Bless you. Sir.'

Right, he thought, immediate crisis over, at least until the next time. Rory knew he shouldn't give out his own money, but things had become so tight for people on the edge and state provision was now so limited that he had given up trying to make emergency claims for people; the service itself had long since stopped any of that and the bureaucracy involved became unmanageable anyway. Sometimes you just have to help, he thought, especially where kids were involved. It wasn't their fault which bed they had been born into and he didn't want them to go hungry.

He left for the meeting, covering for Laura, quickly passing reception.

'I'll see Sophie's lady this afternoon to go through that report. I'm off to that meeting now, back as soon as I can…'

After a short walk he met Shaun Elder as they went into the meeting at Social Services, it was one of the many multi-agency forums that both their organisations attended and the DCI chaired this one. With budget cuts, however, many well-meaning forums had withered. This was a local attempt to combine various functions and share information between agencies. He hoped it would be brisk and had managed to say so to Shaun as they came in and he had agreed. Rory liked the multi-agency support that had been developed in Upper Lowbridge and got on well with most of the police officers he met regularly. He regarded Shaun as a good man.

Some useful information was exchanged on case management and public protection, and agreement reached to give special attention to some cases causing concern and to back off others that were making progress. Rory had taken full notes for Laura.

Tracy O'Marney's case had been mentioned.

'I know the family,' said Shaun. 'I've locked her father up a few times in Longton. From an Irish travelling background, her mother was from a potter's family in Tunstall. Rough as shit both families, oh excuse me. All heavy drinkers, as is her new partner. I'll put a watch marker on the address.' Rory thanked Shaun before returning to the office walking past the Stag and Fawn, but with no time to call in today, unfortunately.

Rory walked through reception where several people were waiting to see him and returned to his desk to a mountain of emails. He did his best to see the offenders who had been waiting for him, providing information, reassurance and guidance in equal measure. After two more phone calls and five urgent emails he was about to get up to make a coffee when reception called to announce the arrival of Sophie's lady.

Oh well, no coffee, he thought, let alone lunch. There was barely time to use the toilet some days! He knew the case vaguely; a high-achieving business woman who was facing sentencing tomorrow for causing death by dangerous driving. Under pressure and busy, she had taken a mobile phone call, missed a red light at a pedestrian crossing and hit a postman on his bike. There was no one else involved but the postman had died at the scene from head injuries. The medical report indicated some vulnerability on his part, but nevertheless there was no doubt that her lack of attention and concentration had caused his death. She had pleaded guilty, the Judge had adjourned for reports and sentencing was due tomorrow, with custody almost inevitable. A suspended sentence in the circumstances was possible, but unlikely.

Rory met the woman and led her to interview room two with a copy of Sophie's report. He sensed her anxiety.

'Will I go to prison, Mr Scott?' she asked. 'And if so for how long?'

'There is no point in pretending other than that will probably be the outcome. I would guess two to five years in the circumstances, probably towards the lower end but let's go through the report, shall we?'

She was an intelligent woman, he handed her a copy and invited her to read it. She did so, shaking and tearful. She asked a few questions about the technicalities and the detail, but accepted that it was a fair and balanced assessment and account of her circumstances and of what had happened. She was desperately sorry, full of remorse and fully prepared to compensate the family of the postman, but none of that would be likely to save her from custody for taking a man's life. Public opinion was putting pressure on the system to treat driving offences where a fatality was involved in a similar way to murder or manslaughter. Nevertheless, under current legislation Rory still felt that two to five years would be the outcome.

Rory checked with her that she had put her affairs in order; made provision for the care of her children with her sister, informed her employer and would leave her house tomorrow with a bag packed of essentials only. It would be likely she would be sent to HMP Foston Hall, just outside Uttoxeter and he explained the basics of what might happen to her there.

She thanked him and left in a calm and dignified manner. Over-use of mobile phones and the distraction from driving safely had become a major problem, Rory reflected. Sad, but people had to take responsibility.

Later that afternoon Sophie made it back to the office and thanked him for covering for her. Laura returned and had to deal with a serious further offence enquiry so Rory just left his notes of the meeting with the DCI in her tray.

Rory had two more court reports allocated to him as he tried to prioritise his outstanding workload. However he looked at it, he was sure it was impossible to complete all that was required in the given timescale. Not unusual, situation normal, he chuckled to himself as he decided which three tasks were the most important and set about addressing them, hoping to finish each of them before close of play today.

His three priorities were: a Crown Court report, a submission to another serious case review and a report to the next Multi Agency Public Protection Panel for a level three case. MAPPA dealt with joint agency planning in the most risky and serious cases and level three was the most serious of those. Not something to get wrong. Two hours of the working day left and three pieces of work that could each easily take a day, he thought. Rory had learnt early in his career how to focus and produce work quickly. He made a coffee before setting about finishing his Crown Court report.

He managed to finish the report with distractions and two more duty interviews by twenty past five. The serious case review document only needed a paragraph adding and then he could start on the MAPPA work. It was six o'clock as he began to eat his lunch. Reception was closed, there was no late night reporting this evening and the phone stopped ringing. Exhausted, by seven o'clock Rory had finished his priority list and got up to leave the building. The light was still on in Laura's office.

He got into his car and started to unwind on the short and pleasant drive from Upper Lowbridge to Millfield. Again, fortunately Bracken had already had his afternoon walk as he greeted him enthusiastically.

'Never mind, boy, we'll have a good walk in the morning,' he said kindly to his ever faithful friend.

Rory looked in the fridge and didn't feel like eating anything on offer. A pint and a sandwich at The Old Plough sounded much more appealing and he was sure that Bracken would agree. He got changed out of his work clothes and into his casual dog-walking gear, which of course Bracken recognised, invoking a spontaneous outburst of tail wagging.

'Come on boy, pub…'

They left the house and set off along the canal bank past the lock and the old lock house. It was still warm and the weather had been dry. The fresh spring air and the steady flow of water always helped Rory to relax. Bracken was also a good grounding influence. Normality resumed and he felt more relaxed; just be your man, his sister had told him and he intended to try to be just that.

* * *

Rory's mobile phone rang in his jacket pocket. He accessed it and looking at the screen saw it was his mother calling.

'Yes, mum, how are you?' Not good it seemed from the shaky tone of her voice when she replied.

'Rory, it's your father, it's serious. He's been taken into hospital; they think he's had a heart attack. Rory, I'm frightened that he's going to die.'

Rory was obviously taken by surprise, shocked, as he kept walking with Bracken running alongside him. What best to do, he wondered? The temptation was to go racing straight off to the hospital, but he paused for thought. 'Let's not panic,' he told himself, 'he's in good hands. There is probably nothing I can actually do to help, other than support mum, so let's not rush into anything.'

By the time they arrived at the pub he knew he would need something to eat. Assuming his father had been taken to the City Hospital in Stoke he knew that it would take him about forty minutes to get there from home, an hour by the time he got back from the walk. Rory managed to remain calm and decided that nothing was likely to change for the next couple of hours so ordered some food at the bar. He then rang his mother back to reassure her and try to find out more information. His mother was struggling to keep her composure but it seemed that his dad had just collapsed at work and someone had seen fit to call an ambulance. From what his mother said, the hospital had managed to stabilise him.

'So which ward is he in at Stoke, mum?'

'No, he's not in Stoke. We're staying with friends in Bath this week while he's working down here and he's been taken to Bristol Royal Infirmary… you will come won't you?'

'Yes of course I will,' he said thinking, *Bristol!*

Rory munched his food down and set off for home as quickly as he could. He fed Bracken and left him in the house, checked the map quickly and set off for the motorway. It was eight thirty as he drove off on his mercy mission to see his father and support his mother. He wondered what Emma was doing but didn't want to delay further to ring her.

The M6 was relatively clear as Rory drove down the outside lane at ninety towards the M5 and down towards Bristol. Was his mother being over dramatic he wondered in saying that his father might die? That would be unlike her, he thought. People survived heart attacks these days, didn't they, he concluded?

All sorts of mixed thoughts and emotions went through his mind as he hurtled down the fast lane. What would he feel if his father did die? How might his mum cope? How might he cope with his mum not coping? Rory admitted to himself that he had never really considered such eventualities before.

His phone rang several times but he couldn't answer it; he did glance enough, however, to see that it was his sister trying to ring him. Not enough time to stop, he thought.

It was eleven thirty as Rory pulled into the hospital car park wondering what he would find. He followed the pedestrian signs to reception whilst accessing his phone for missed calls. His sister had asked if he was going to the hospital, she said she couldn't as she was about to board a plane for Paris. His mother was pressing him to know when he was going to arrive.

Reception was closed, so Rory opted to head for the

49

acute medical ward. Staff told him that his father was still in A&E, but when he found his way there staff told him that his father had been transferred to the cardiac unit.

As Rory tramped along seemingly endless hospital corridors, he wondered what he would find. The unit was still busy at that time of night, as he approached the front desk.

'Hi, I'm Rory Scott, my father's with you following a heart attack. How is he?'

'His name?'

'Michael Scott.'

'Oh yes, he's in bed twelve, Sir. I'll ask the nurse who is looking after him to speak to you.'

'Can you just tell me an outline?'

'No not really.'

Rory choose not to argue and went to find bed twelve and soon found his mother sitting next to the bed. As he approached, not really knowing what to expect, his mother looked up, relieved to see him.

'Oh, Rory, bless you, you're here. He's sleeping soundly now,' she said as she got up to embrace him.

'Will he be alright, mum?'

'Oh I do hope so, darling. They've told me that the next twenty-four hours are critical but that they've done all they can and are hopeful for a full recovery.'

'That's good; do you believe them?'

'Well they all seem so young, but what can we do but trust them. It should be alright, dear.'

Rory looked at his father with care, compassion and concern. He felt that he looked peaceful and at rest, which he assumed was a good thing. He was connected to a variety of tubes and machines busily monitoring every possible indicator from blood pressure to heartbeat and recording every detail from his date of birth to his blood group. Rory glanced at the indicators, not taking much notice. He leaned forward to touch his hand and his dad opened his eyes for a moment, murmured then went immediately back to sleep.

The nurse allocated to his father arrived and introduced herself and reassured them about his prospects before rushing off to assist a patient needing immediate critical care. Rory looked up at his mum who suddenly looked so tired and strained; for the first time Rory felt he saw a degree of vulnerability from someone he had always known as being so stoic, so strong and so resilient.

Chapter Fourteen

As Rory drove away from the hospital feeling a little guilty about leaving his mother, he glanced at his watch, it was just past one o'clock in the morning and even at this time of night he faced a good two-hour drive back to Millfield. Rory braced himself to manage with little sleep, knowing that he had to be in the office by eight. He needed to prepare for an important meeting with the police and Children's Services about another case they were jointly involved in. They needed to share information to inform their risk assessments before taking any further action. The case hung in the balance; critically they had to decide whether removing the children or arresting the father and instigating a breach proceeding against him was likely to result in the best chance of stabilising the family and avoiding potential disaster. Rory liked these cases, with the challenge of really making a difference if you got it right, but he was also acutely aware of the likely consequences if you got it wrong. He knew that the media would likely jump to conclusions and inevitably blame the agencies. It was also no good banking on support from his own organisation, who he felt would just as easily hang him out to dry.

The motorway was clear as Rory speeded north. He calculated that he could make the journey in good time. What would happen, he thought, how would his father recover and how was he going to get through the following day? As he approached Millfield he knew that an anxious dog would be waiting. Rory parked up, thankful to have made it home, opened the door to much tail wagging and excitement. He felt that Bracken was talking to him without words, expressing his joy and relief, not enquiring about the reasons why his master was so late, but just glad to see him.

It took a while to calm Bracken down before he could pull back the duvet and try to get some sleep. It was a few minutes past four. He set the alarm for seven. Thankfully the following three hours provided deep and refreshing sleep so Rory didn't feel too jaded as he eased out of bed to face the morning. The thought struck him that this was normal for some of his colleagues with young children so he shouldn't complain.

Rory got ready quickly, arranged for one of the others in the house to walk Bracken and set off to work. He drove carefully through the morning traffic along the familiar route to Upper Lowbridge. As he sat down at his desk Rory had quite forgotten about his forthcoming meeting, but felt confident about his knowledge of the case. He quickly went through the records and made a few notes of the key points to avoid, taking the file with him. Too many files had been lost over the years and Rory made it his business to avoid that practice unless he was meeting in his own building.

Joseph smiled as they exchanged nods. He noticed that Rory looked a little strained but was assured as Rory gave him the thumbs up before slurping his last drop of coffee and heading off to Social Services. Sergeant Becky Jackson was already there waiting in reception when he arrived.

'Toni isn't in yet, but is expected any time now, just take a seat,' announced the receptionist with practised ease. Where would you like me to take it, thought Rory in response to the ambiguous invitation? He and Becky exchanged glances and smiled as they both knew social workers' reputations for poor punctuality. They talked about other cases and Rory told her about his father's heart attack and she expressed her sympathy.

The efficient receptionist in what was a large multi-use building approached them and let them through the security barrier, pointed out the coffee machine and confirmed that they were booked into meeting room three. The two officers took their coffee and sat down. Fortunately, it wasn't long before a flustered Toni Gray crashed through the door muttering something about last-minute child care arrangements. She quickly sat down and they focussed on the matter in hand.

'Toni, do you want to start with your perception of the situation at home?' suggested Becky.

'OK. Sonia has made some real improvements, but struggles to maintain them. She tells me that she is currently off the drugs and I have no evidence to dispute that,' she reported as Becky smiled knowingly.

'The house is much cleaner and the school is reporting improvement in all three children's behaviour, general appearance and attitude in school. This has reduced the pressure on them of isolation and bullying. Other children can be very cruel if some of their number appear to be unkempt or smelly. The greater concern though is the return of the boyfriend Jack, who we know can be violent. That raises concern about the safety of both Sonia and the children. Sonia hasn't reported any incidents to me this week but she's not always reliable in that regard, especially when Jack is threatening her to keep quiet.'

'I smiled,' responded Becky, 'when you mentioned drugs. Sonia has been seen regularly including yesterday afternoon at the address of a well-known local supplier we have under surveillance. She's either; using drugs herself, or dealing or collecting the stuff to pass on to Jack.'

'OK. Jack is subject to regular drug testing as part of his licence and is due for a test tomorrow, so we'll know if she's collecting for him, or at least whether he's using,' added Rory.

'I'll put a marker out for any reports of domestic violence at that address. So far there have only been a couple of calls from a neighbour about shouting and disturbance. So what do we think, guys, act now or continue to monitor?' posed Becky.

'It's got to be monitor at this stage, hasn't it really?' said Toni and the others agreed.

Notes were tidied up and actions set with the expectation of another meeting soon when the drugs test results were available. If that resulted in breach for Jack then the pressure on the whole family would ease.

They all got up quickly, said their goodbyes and rushed off. Rory was feeling tired now, but he knew that he had to get through the day. Before he got back to the office he thought he would just ring the hospital to check on progress with his father. When he got through to the ward the news was not what he expected.

'I'm very sorry to have to tell you, Mr Scott, but your father died thirty minutes ago and we were just about to ring you. He passed away unexpectedly in his sleep.'

Shocked, he stuttered, 'Does my mother know yet?' he asked.

'No, we've been unable to contact her. Her mobile is switched off and that's the only number we have.'

Rory said a notional thank you, didn't feel that there was anything more to be said and told the nurse that he would inform his mother. He assumed that she must have gone home after he had left. It was approaching ten o'clock so she may well still be asleep. This was not to be done by phone he thought. I need to visit. With a heavy heart and mixed emotions Rory returned to the office, called in to see Laura and arranged to take the rest of the day off to go and visit his mother and start making all the necessary arrangements. He just had time to tell Joseph as he left who seemed genuinely moved and offered to cover for him. All his feelings of ambivalence towards his father, his sense of unease associated with him all churned around in his mind, mixed with sadness, guilt and regret.

* * *

Rory approached his parents' house on the edge of Uttoxeter and could see that the lights were now on. As he pulled off the lane and into the drive, he could see his mother through the reception room window in her dressing gown. As he got out of the car the front door opened and she approached him with open arms.

'Darling, how kind of you to come to see me, can you

stay long? I'm just about to ring the hospital for a progress report, he's on the mend now. I've been thinking about persuading your father to retire, it's clearly for the best, this is a warning and life is too short to ignore it...!' she pronounced rambling at great speed.

'Mum, we had better go inside,' he replied calmly.

'Well don't you agree; he will get a good pension after all. We could travel or even live abroad, you wouldn't mind would you, darling, he always wanted to do that.'

They went into the house with his mother still expressing her well-intended plans, and as she went to put the kettle on, Rory's phone rang. It was Emma.

'Rory, I've just heard, I'm devastated. Where are you?'

'I'm at mum's.'

'Does she know yet?'

'No, I'm about to tell her.'

'OK, I'm on my way, I'm in Manchester. I'll be with you by lunch time.'

'Now dear, you do realise that you and Emma might have to take some time off to help your father recover, don't you?' his mother stated firmly while placing a tray of tea on the kitchen table.

'Mum, please sit down.'

'There's lot to do, Rory, no time for that – have you had your breakfast, what time do you want lunch?'

Exasperated, Rory felt he had no choice but to tell her bluntly, 'Mum, the situation has changed; dad's not going to recover...' He took a deep breath: 'Mum, he died early this morning in hospital.'

Stunned silence fell as she sat down.

'Oh dear, all those plans, all those hopes, oh dear, all gone in an instant...'

Rory tried to comfort his mother as best he could. She was pleased to hear that Emma was on her way. After the initial shock, tears followed and then anxious planning for recovery turned to the practical consideration of funeral arrangements.

'He'd want flowers. Dress: all in black, of course,

burial not cremation. Shall we ask Emerys dear, yes of course, Emerys, it will have to be Emerys and catering by Jenkinsons. Hymns dear…'

'Mother, sit down it doesn't have to be all done this instant.'

'Some of those families you know, they will take the clothes won't they? I'm sure they would be grateful, he always had good clothes, your father… your father…' she said, suddenly looking drawn as more tears returned.

Rory looked at her with a moment's hesitation.

'Rory, Rory my dear, you were always so precious to us, darling, you know that don't you?'

Confused Rory asked, 'What do you mean? What are you trying to say, mother?'

'Oh darling, he never wanted you to know, he insisted on it, but now you will find out anyway won't you?'

'Find out what, mother?'

'Didn't you notice his blood group? I saw you looking at the monitor in the hospital.'

'Yes, but what of it?' replied Rory, not yet making the connection.

'That your father wasn't your real father after all,' she spluttered. 'You were adopted, darling…'

PART TWO

Chapter Fifteen

Becky was chasing the lead with Barclays Bank, trying to extract information about Donald York's accounts. They weren't being particularly helpful, and she had to be assertive to get through to someone with sufficient authority to potentially sanction her having access to any information that might be remotely useful. The bank manager agreed to research old records after Becky had politely reminded him of his responsibilities to cooperate with the police in such circumstances and that should he fail to do so she could confiscate all necessary records herself. He rang her back within an hour.

'Sergeant Jackson, it's me – the person you spoke to at the bank. I can verify that there is a pattern of large deposits going into Mr York's account and significant sums being paid to the religious charity you mentioned. The money coming in is paid from an account used by the radio station at that time for donations from viewers to various charity appeals, including supporting Auldbeck. It may interest you to know that there is a discrepancy between the amounts paid into the charity and those subsequently paid out to good causes of between twenty and thirty per cent per transaction.'

'Thank you, that's very helpful.' So he was creaming off money for himself as well as using donations to effectively buy the children. What a thoroughly horrible man! Next step, she thought, was to chase up any links with the charity and see if their receipts matched York's payments, to verify what the bank had reported. Perhaps the bank manager would assist her, now that he had discovered how to be helpful? Becky was due to meet with Shaun later that day to review progress before reporting to the ACC, so she was pleased that things were moving.

* * *

Shaun was reading the pathologist's report as Becky entered his office. Her phone rang. It was the bank reporting that on closer inspection there were other payments going out of the radio station's charity account that didn't appear to be going to good causes and might warrant further investigation?

'Hi, Becky, have you any news?'

'Yes, Sir. The financial picture confirms money coming into the radio station charity appeals account, then on to Auldbeck and other charities but also that he was creaming off twenty to thirty per cent – the bastard,' reported Becky.

'Was he now? Interesting, well done, Becky. I'm just reading the pathology report. The doctor confirms that the body in the garden was female, estimated to be between three and five years old and that death was consistent with strangulation, no more given the age and condition of the body. He can't formally identify her as Molly Bennett but the circumstantial evidence is very strong. He's still waiting for the DNA test results to see how closely the body matches Molly's brother,' responded Shaun.

'That sounds good to me. It's got to be her, don't you think?'

'Yes, I agree, but it may not satisfy a court. The search team found no more bodies in the house or garden by the way,' concluded Shaun.

The officers were able to report their good news to the ACC, who expressed some satisfaction with their progress.

* * *

The next day heralded an important development and potential breakthrough; a witness had come forward.

Harold Oldfield was born in the nearest village to York's cottage and was walking his dog on the day that Molly disappeared. Harold was only twelve at the time, but he reported distinctly remembering hearing shouting coming from the cottage as he walked past. It didn't really make sense to him at the time and his mother had told him to mind his own business and not to tell tales, but it had bothered him all his life. When he heard that a body had been found in the cottage garden he had immediately gone to the police to report his recollections and concerns.

Harold said in his statement that he remembered hearing a child crying and screaming 'no, no, no'. He was sure it was a girl's cry. He also remembered a man's voice saying 'you will'.

For DCI Shaun Elder, instinct told him that he was now investigating a murder following a sexual assault and probably attempted rape and that was how the poor girl had died, either fitting or strangled or probably both as she fought to resist being raped. How awful. It simply further added to his determination to see York put away for as long as possible, for life if he could make a murder charge stick.

Chapter Sixteen

Rory was reeling from his mother's revelation. He felt that he should leave before making any comment that he may regret later; he wanted to be alone, to reflect, to try to absorb what he had just been told. He felt such a mixture of emotions; devastation, anger, disappointment and of being let down. How could his parents have maintained this facade for all these years and more importantly, why, for what purpose? As he thought about it driving home he also felt an emerging sense of almost relief, yes relief. Could this explain, or go towards explaining, why he had always felt different, why he had always felt that he didn't fit in? Why oh why had they not told him? That was the part he was struggling with most. Could he ever forgive them, he thought?

Rory got home and was pleased with Bracken's unknowing but reassuring welcome, a sense of normality and an opportunity to walk the familiar canal bank beckoned. He could let his thoughts run. He had felt tired but now was energised. He walked, he wondered; memories, questions, thoughts. Regrets and anger. In some ways Rory felt robbed, robbed of the opportunity ever to confront his father, to tell him what he thought of him, robbed of a childhood, robbed of his very identity.

Rory sat quietly at home that evening. It was cool so he lit the fire. The warmth from his log burner helped to ease his pain. He opened a bottle of beer and another. Later he composed an email to send to Laura, his Line Manager, requesting some compassionate leave. He had already told her that his father had died but didn't mention his news of his own adoption in his note. Nevertheless, he needed some space and there was a funeral to organise. That could be a focus now, to mourn the loss of his now adopted father and in some ways his own childhood. As the evening wore on with more beers Rory decided that he needed to see his mother tomorrow, to seek some explanation, some context. Yes that would be what he would do, he thought.

The next morning, after walking Bracken, Rory set off to his mother's house. He tried to stay calm as he drove, tried to remind himself that for his mother her concentration would be on the loss of her husband and that for her the revelation to him would probably be a mere side issue. She had also been rambling, so Rory was not optimistic about getting very far, at least not today.

When he arrived he could see his sister's car parked in the drive. It would be good to see her. As he entered the house the atmosphere was already tense. Emma greeted him saying that their mother was driving her to distraction, flitting around all over the place, making unnecessary and unrealistic demands and being difficult as she was minded to be at times. Mother appeared still in her dressing gown, as he had left her it seemed, crying, almost wailing.

'Oh, Rory, darling, my dear boy, how pleased I am to see you. Emma is being obstructive, as usual and not helping. You will help, darling, won't you? Have you made all the arrangements with Emery's yet? We will need them to collect your father's body. They do that, I assume?'

Rory was so tempted to pitch in straight away with 'yes but he was not my father, was he', but resisted.

'See what I mean, Rory?' said Emma.

'Mum, come on this is difficult for all of us but we need to all be tolerant of each other at a time like this.'

'Oh, Rory, you are so understanding and diplomatic! No wonder you're a probation officer. I've been telling her to stop being an arse all morning!' replied his sister.

'OK, Emma, not now. Mum, after what you told me yesterday I really haven't thought about Emery's or, if I'm honest, the body,' Rory replied.

'Yes well you know now, darling. So now that is dealt with, we can all concentrate on the funeral.'

'Told him what, mother? Told him what?' said Emma.

'Oh, hasn't she said?' Rory replied.

'Said what? Stop talking in riddles!' said Emma getting exasperated.

'Emma, yesterday mum let slip that dad was not my real father. She told me that I had been adopted.'

'What!' cried Emma. 'Mother, how could you! You mean Rory was adopted and you never told him, you never told either of us!'

'Well. It wasn't important at the time, dear,' her mother replied.

'She said dad insisted that I never knew and now that he's gone, she let it slip.'

'Oh, mother...' said Emma, sinking into a chair in tears with her head in her hands.

'Oh don't worry, darling, you weren't adopted, it was only dear Rory,' said her mother in a pitiful attempt at damage limitation.

'So that makes it OK then does it?' responded Emma rhetorically.

'Well quite, darling,' missing her point completely.

Both children glared at her in disbelief, demanding more.

Mother sat down and tried to explain.

'You see your father always wanted a boy and after you were born, Emma, I found that I couldn't have any more children, to give him what he wanted – so he suggested that we adopted one. In those days the process was easy and there were plenty of babies available, so that's what we did...'

'Oh great, so you didn't really want me and you adopted him... weren't you meant to tell him, as he grew up I mean?' challenged Emma.

'Oh yes, darling, but your father insisted you see.'

'And you never challenged him?'

'Well of course not, darling, he was your father.'

* * *

Arrangements were eventually made for a funeral which

passed off as a strained but polite affair, with their mother rising to the occasion to keep up appearances. Rory had declined her invitation to deliver a eulogy, which she seemed to fail to grasp was now clearly inappropriate. Rory never really liked his father and at least now he didn't need to pretend anymore.

Chapter Seventeen

On his return to work people were kind to him, although very quickly his news was forgotten, about his father's death at least. Rory had chosen not to announce his adoption publically but to tell people individually as the opportunity arose.

Rory initially threw himself back into work, hoping to just get on with it. Donald York's case was proving to be absorbing and therefore useful in that respect. On remand at HMP Downgate, it seemed he was adjusting to his new circumstances. Rory had been made aware of developments in the police investigation by Becky and was due to visit York in prison himself to try to gain some insight from his point of view. While Becky and Shaun would no doubt try to secure a confession to murder.

In Downgate, initially York was finding his way around the criminal world. He had quickly learned that life inside is fairly stark unless you arrange to maximise opportunities to bring things in to provide some comfort either within or outside the rules. Traditional items such as tobacco and chocolate were still currency but drugs and mobile phones were the things to have to buy influence or protection. York was used to influencing and manipulating people, and staff and prisoners alike soon cottoned on to his celebrity status, such that in the vulnerable prisoners' wing he soon became universally referred to by his radio name, as Mr Chas.

Mr Chas found that staff in a modern private prison could be enterprising in their own right. Wages and conditions of service were poor, there was a hire and fire mentality and most staff didn't seem to expect or receive loyalty from the organisation or give it in return. Some staff quite openly responded to 'shopping lists'. Once he had acquired a mobile phone, York could easily arrange for payment to be made to staff from outside and he started to build his alliances. He recognised the potential in one young female officer who was struggling as a single parent. Once she had succumbed to his generous offer in return for first bringing in cigars, she had crossed the Rubicon. Hidden in her bra to avoid detection when being searched entering the prison she felt that she had found access to easy money with minimum risk of being caught. More requests followed and she quickly was beyond the point of no return. To withdraw her service would lead to exposure and no doubt dismissal so she carried on until the inevitable happened and she was caught smuggling into her own establishment. Mr Chas didn't see the officer again after that, but he soon found a substitute.

This brought him to the attention of some of the more powerful prisoners and one in particular took exception to his apparent special status and decided to muscle in on the act.

Mr Chas found himself summoned to a meeting and offered terms with no negotiation. He was to accept 'protection' and use his money and influence to arrange for items to be brought in on demand. Under threat, other prisoners would hold items if required or if a search was likely with the understanding that should anything be found the poor unfortunate prisoners holding the goods would readily claim that they were theirs, knowing that whatever punishment the prison may enforce would be nothing compared to the retribution metered out by the bullies.

In reviewing security arrangements with the Prison Director, the Head of Security remained concerned about several areas including staff collusion and the evident presence of mobile phones. The Director had been working with a telecom company for some time exploring the possibility of moving beyond use of equipment that could detect a mobile signal and its location. He wanted to block all mobile communication within a certain radius of the prison estate. If that could be implemented, then in a stroke the initiative would be back with the authorities and mobile phones in the prison would be rendered useless.

That would be both a major security victory and a significant career marker for the Director.

At the same time prisoners had found the use of drones offered considerable scope for smuggling. They could drop contraband over the prison fence, or directly to cell windows at night largely undetected. As well as acquiring the contraband there was the sense of glee in knowing that the prison authorities were aware that it was happening but seemed unable to stop it. Perversely it almost resembled a drive-through fast food outlet. Prisoners delighted in the 'call and collect' service that they had managed to establish.

In the early days of this technology, night flights became common with the capacity to bring in a whole range of barred items; whole phones, chargers, alcohol, drugs, pornography and weapons were all on the preferred shopping list top ten. Such a sudden influx of these items had the ability to destabilise a prison rapidly, allowing it to descend into violence, intimidation and chaos. As fast as the authorities were able to find contraband, more simply arrived to take its place. A more radical solution was needed and needed fast.

The Director met with the Head of Security to review the matter.

'OK, Mick, tell me what's happening?' the Director enquired.

'Well, Sir, it's not good, we risk losing control here. The volume of drugs and weapons floating around the place has got out of hand.'

'We are talking knives here presumably?' asked the Director, for confirmation.

'Oh no, Sir, it's much worse than that. We've found two machetes already and I wonder how long it will be before they bring in firearms. A drone could easily handle the weight of a pistol.'

'OK,' replied the Director sombrely. 'I'll need to talk to the Area Manager about this. In the meantime, let's see if we can at least hang some big nets over the cell windows from the outside to stop ingress. After that the solution has got to be a tech one, don't you think? We need to stop the wretched things flying.'

'Yes, Sir.'

* * *

DCI Shaun Elder and Sergeant Becky Jackson arrived at Downgate to interview Donald York in connection with the possible murder of Molly Bennett for the second time. As before, York was brought to them in an interview room in the visits hall.

York looked worried as he sat down in front of the officers.

'Mr York, we now have evidence from Pathology that confirms the body in the garden as female and of Molly Bennett's age. The report also suggests death by strangulation.'

'No, no she was screaming, became hysterical, I was trying to calm her down.'

'What by stopping her breathing?'

'No by holding my hand over her mouth, someone could have heard her.'

'They did, Mr York. We have a witness that heard a child screaming "no" and a man saying "you will". How do you account for that, Mr York?'

He covered his face with his hands.

'I never intended for her to die, DCI Elder, honestly I didn't.'

'Mr York, I am still waiting for further test results but I fully anticipate charging you with the murder of Molly Bennett very shortly. I suggest that you need to think about that. You are not a young man and your only route to any prospect of eventual release would be to shorten your sentence as far as possible. A confession would allow the Judge to reduce your minimum term; you will get a life sentence but the minimum term could be a short as ten years in the circumstances, but if you force a trial and lose it will be much longer.'

'Confess to murder, Chief Inspector?'
    'Precisely.'

Chapter Eighteen

The house in Millfield was the old vicarage, a Victorian three-storey town house style property standing in its own grounds. The front garden over the years had been either sold off in lots or used to extend the car park. At the rear, an old orchard remained next to large lawned area and a vegetable patch that had seen better days. It was a lovely house now converted into flats and shared living space with single or double rooms.

When Rory had finished his degree and secured his first job he didn't want to return to live with his parents so had taken a single room in the top floor of the house. The other five rooms were all occupied by single people and a young couple. The kitchen, two bathrooms, a shower room and the living / dining area were all shared. Well-behaved animals were allowed. Rory was delighted to be able to have a dog of his own, something he always wanted and that his father had never allowed.

The other occupants were all friendly and pleasant people, who more than accommodated each other – except perhaps for Jo who was very private, moody and somewhat serious. Most of the group had willingly joined in and made the best of the opportunity of shared living. They cooked together sometimes and shared the chores, although the girls would claim, quite rightly, that mostly the boys didn't play their part. They did, however, chop wood for the stove and help in other ways. Bracken always had someone to walk him if Rory couldn't and he provided an element of security. The girls said they felt safer in the house on their own if Bracken was around.

Rory didn't feel in any rush to 'settle down'. He hadn't found the love of his life and was very content, for now, with this communal and affordable existence. His parents didn't either understand or 'approve', but he didn't care. This was a comfortable and affordable lifestyle that suited him, at least for now. Rory did think that he might enjoy a family life of his own at some point, although recent events cast doubt in his mind about even the thought of such an eventuality. How could he possibly be prepared to nurture the next generation after his own childhood experience, he thought?

Investment in those relationships paid dividends for Rory when the news broke of his loss and family revelation. The whole house was shocked, very sympathetic and supportive in those vital early days of reeling from recent events. He appreciated the support and was able to talk openly and express his feelings; the mixed emotions around the loss of his adopted father, the anger, the hurt, and the disappointment.

As he returned from walking Bracken along the canal Rory was conscious that he had promised to ring Laura today to keep her informed of his intentions. He had taken three days' compassionate leave, some time owing him and had booked a week of annual leave. After that he wasn't sure. Suddenly, work seemed less important, even remote, another life belonging to someone else. He rang Laura, standing by the canal bridge overlooking farm fields with the morning sun on his back, enjoying the warmth of late spring. Bracken ran back and forth trying to trace any signs of rabbits, recognising that the small black box held to his master's ear signalled that they may be a while.

'Thanks for ringing, Rory; firstly and most importantly, how are you?' she asked with genuine concern.

'Still shocked, I guess, Laura. I feel like I've been in a car crash and am shaken, battered and bruised. I'm still quite numb really.'

'How's your mother?' she asked.

'I don't know. I haven't spoken to her since the funeral.'

'Is that wise?'

'Probably not, but I haven't got the energy at the moment.'

'OK, so I'm sorry to be practical, Rory, but what are

your plans?'

'I suppose I haven't got any, but I know that doesn't help you. My leave extends for another week and then I'm due back at work.'

'You could take sick leave if you don't feel ready, or… Rory, I know I've mentioned this before, but the staff counselling scheme can be very helpful, I've used it myself. We do want you back, Rory, but most of all we all want you to be well, so you take your time and you decide. Just let me know.'

'Thanks, Laura… I will. I do appreciate it.'

Bracken looked up as soon as the phone went back into his master's pocket as if to say, 'can we carry on now'?

'Yes, OK,' replied Rory setting off back to the house. Maybe I should seek help, he thought. One thing he had learnt from his upbringing was a sense of pride in independence and self-reliance, so like many men the notion of acknowledging his own frailties was difficult for Rory. They stepped through the gate and back onto the lane towards the house, past the pub and the church. The church was still used for occasional Sunday services but mostly for weddings now, which had become ever more elaborate and dominated the village on most Saturdays during the summer season. He was aware that he needed to make a decision on what to do next. Rory was fairly decisive, but this was new territory for him. At this stage, he kept reminding himself, it was entirely reasonably to feel shocked and numb, but he desperately wanted to avoid paralysis.

Over the following few days Rory talked to his housemates and to Emma and recognised that he was secure, lucky in many ways, housed and fed and had a job. His responsibility was to the community he served, he thought. Returning to work would help him focus, not get too self-indulgent. After all, coming to terms with his new status was not going to happen overnight. So that was it, he would go back to work, he decided.

Chapter Nineteen

The DNA results were received. The analysis concluded that there was a DNA match between the skeleton and Molly Bennett's brother, confirming the identity of the body in the garden. Given all the other indicators and circumstantial evidence, Shaun was confident that he could now proceed. He could charge York with murder and he felt that the CPS would run with it. He arranged to go back to HMP Downgate.

The ACC was pleased and thanked him and his team for their efforts. Shaun felt relieved and vindicated, at least so far, but he was aware that the process was far from over. As he and Becky arrived at the prison, he wondered how York would react. He wasn't sure. In fact their meeting was over in a few minutes. Presented with the evidence, York crumbled into tears and admitted that he was complicit in Molly's death.

'She became hysterical, then started coughing and panting, as if she couldn't breathe. I tried to hold her down but she resisted. Then she started to fight back, to subdue her I held her neck…'

'Do you mean throat, Mr York, did you strangle her?'

'No, no, I held her throat to stop her hitting me. Then when she had stopped I realised that she had died in my arms,' he said sobbing.

'Did you try to rape her, Mr York?'

'No no, I wouldn't do that.'

'But you did kill her?'

'I suppose so, yes…'

'Donald York, I am charging you with the murder of Molly Bennett, you do not need to say anything but…'

The words just seemed to fade away as York stopped listening, knowing that the truth had finally come out.

'Do you think he was trying to rape her, Sir?' asked Becky as they left the prison.

'Hard to say. There is no suggestion of going beyond

sexual assault in any of the other cases. I guess we will never know. In any event, I'll take that as a confession to murder, whatever it was he was trying to do to that poor child.'

Chapter Twenty

Back at work, Rory tried hard to recover his enthusiasm for the job but he just felt drained. Maybe he should have had more time off? He didn't know.

He caught up with developments in the Donald York case and no further reports of domestic violence had been received from Sonia. Her boyfriend Jack had been recalled while Rory had been off, for further non-compliance with his licence conditions. The lady in the 'death by dangerous driving' case was still awaiting sentence. New tasks were allocated and interesting new priorities emerged, but it was a struggle. The others in the team were supportive to a point, but they all had their own problems and a heavy workload to keep them more than busy.

At times, even with people around him, Rory did feel quite lonely. Maybe it was right to talk to a counsellor, at least then as Laura had said it would be his time without interruption. He decided he would seek an appointment and was pleased to find accessing the service to be easy and secured a first meeting for the following week for an initial assessment. As he mulled over his feelings, a whole further area of concern started to unfold for him. After the anger and feelings of being deceived it suddenly occurred to him if the man who had brought him up was not in fact his father, then who was? He had no idea. What was his real family background? Given that he wasn't like his adopted parents, did he resemble his real parents? He felt like he was in a void. Who am I, he suddenly began to wonder? He didn't even know his real name.

Over the next few weeks with reflection and the help of the counsellor, Rory started to address some of these concerns and explore some approaches as to how he might deal with them. He was informed that Social Services kept records of such matters long-term and that he could apply to seek some basic information about his real family. Firstly, however, he had to consider what he might discover and whether or not he really wanted to know. Would it make him feel any easier? He wasn't sure.

Taking advice from others, Rory was aware that for counselling to be effective you have to buy into it and be clear about what you are trying to achieve. The counsellor had been very helpful in explaining how she worked and in trying to establish an early bond of trust between them. Rory's initial impression was that he could work with this woman. He thought about his intentions and tried to talk them through with her. He supposed that he just wanted to express his feelings about the shock of hearing that he had been adopted and be able to put that emotion to one side. Then to work through the implications and the questions he needed to answer to unravel the truth about his family history.

The counsellor was very reassuring and encouraging about the approach Rory was taking. She told him that many people take months or even years to reach that point.

Rory didn't come to any firm resolution quickly but was grateful for the chance to talk openly and think about some of the issues involved. If he was able to find out more about his real family, would it satisfy his curiosity or simply lead to more questions that he could not answer? If he could actually trace them, would they want to know him? He could face simply compounding his sense of rejection and isolation if they didn't. Rory made some tentative enquires with Social Services who reassured him that adoption records were kept safe and some information should be available but that he was right to be cautious and think through how he might react to what he might find. He decided to probe his mother for information first although he was sceptical about how much she might know, let alone be prepared to share with him.

He arranged to see her after work one evening and stay for dinner. She was still grieving herself of course and feeling more than a little guilty for the impact on Rory of her silence over all those years.

After a while he broached the subject, 'Mother, I want

to talk about my adoption.'

'Oh must we, darling?'

'Yes, you owe me that at least,' he replied as she turned away. 'Mum, I want to know all you know about my real family. I want to know where I came from, I want to discover a sense of my own identity.'

'Yes, dear, would you like some tea?'

'Oh come on, mum, don't try to fob me off, I need to know, please.'

'It was a long time ago, Rory. We didn't ask many questions, your father and I, and the nuns didn't either. They were satisfied that we could offer a loving home to a child. We asked for a baby boy and after a while they contacted us and said they had one.'

'Go on,' Rory probed.

'Well that was about it then, I gather it's much more complicated now but on the day we had you one of the nuns simply came to call and handed us this baby. You were two days old, well dressed and wrapped in a blue blanket. You had a teddy bear with you and that was all.'

'Where is the bear now, mother?' asked Rory grasping at any potential link with his past.

'Oh don't be silly, darling, that was nearly thirty years ago. I have no idea!'

OK, he thought, maybe that was unreasonable, and he smiled trying to lighten the atmosphere.

'Do you remember anything about my parents?'

'No not much, darling, just that I think they were two single university students.'

'Do you remember a name?'

'Rory was the name they had given you and we liked it so we kept it. It was the name of the hospital ward consultant where you were born'

'No, mother, do you remember their names, or at least my real surname?'

'Oh I see, umm… Carpenter I think.'

Carpenter, Rory thought, well maybe my ancestors were tradesmen then? It's not a bad name, he thought. His mother changed the subject and he thought that was probably as much as he was likely to extract from her now so he turned his attention to dinner.

'What's for dinner then, mum?' he asked.

'Roast beef, Rory, your father's favourite!'

* * *

After a while back at work Rory was looking forward to his next leave that he had booked months ago for a mid-summer break. Emma had offered to go away with him and had suggested a canal barge holiday. She reasoned that Rory would enjoy the outdoor experience, walking along the towpath and that the fresh air and being out of a stuffy office would do them both good. It would also be nice to be able to take Bracken along. She had researched it thoroughly and found a hire place not far from where Rory lived. When she had rung him to suggest it he was really pleased both at the prospect of a break, but also to have time with his sister.

'Rory, do you know the canal shop and boat hire place at Great Haywood? It sounds just right. I've been on their website, Anglo Welsh Waterways Holidays and they do all sizes of boats and help you plan routes, as obviously you can only go in one direction and then have to turn round somewhere allowing the timings to fit with your holiday and to return the boat to where you started.'

'Vaguely,' he replied. 'Yes I really fancy that; cooked breakfasts, walks with Bracken and pub lunches. Are you sure you could handle the boat if I'm walking alongside?' he enquired and could sense his sister sighing.

'Yes of course I am. I'm a better driver than you anyway. You can man the kitchen! Shall I book it then for that week in June?'

'Yes please, Emma, that would be great and it's very kind of you.'

'Don't kid yourself, I'm trying to be helpful, don't say that's a first, but I really want to go too and have never had anyone to go with. It will be nice to spend some time together.'

Settled then, Rory felt more relaxed and contented than he had for a while. A week on a boat with his fun-loving sister! That was something to look forward to.

Chapter Twenty-One

The CPS confirmed that they were prepared to proceed with the prosecution of Donald York for the murder of Molly Bennett and for two further counts of sexual assault against her and her brother. Given that York had already made what was effectively a confession in front of two police officers a trial was avoided and the Judge was free to call for reports ready for sentencing. Behind the scenes, York's counsel were still arguing for the lesser charges.

Rory started writing his report promptly, having already researched the case, had a brief telephone conversation with Bill, Molly Bennett's brother and interviewed Donald York in prison. Given that murder carried a mandatory life sentence, Rory knew that he was not influencing the Judge's decision on the outcome, but that his report would form an important body of analysis and opinion throughout his sentence and in any future deliberations by the Parole Board on potential release on life licence. The Judge of course retained discretion on the all-important question of tariff. That is the minimum term to be served before any consideration of release. In York's case Rory guessed it was likely to be at least ten years and could well be a long as fifteen. Given his age, in either event it was questionable whether York would survive long enough for release to even be considered, but as the DCI had advised him, his guilty plea gave him his best chance.

A guilty plea of course was such a relief for family members of the victim who would not have to endure the rigours of a trial, as Rory was also well aware. Culpability was already accepted and decided.

Rory carefully laid out in his report the context of the offences, the deliberate nature of targeting vulnerable children and the financial aspect with siphoning off payments to the charity, the likely number of victims involved, the length of time during which his activities had taken place and the likely degree of lasting damage to those concerned. Donald York's somewhat reluctant degree of acceptance of responsibility, of limited insight into his behaviour and of little regret and remorse were also pertinent considerations. Apart from the nature of the offences, Rory could not detect any particular vulnerability, or risk of self-harm or suicide to warn the prison authorities about. He could also advise the Judge of the likely accredited programmes that York would be expected to engage in designed to improve his understanding of the impact of his actions, the reasons why he acted as he did and to reduce the likelihood of any reoccurrence.

Rory anticipated York being moved to HMP Stafford or HMP Whatton following conviction. If he was at Stafford, Rory speculated whether he may work with him directly if he was seconded to the prison service at some point in his career over the next few years.

When he finished work that day Rory felt like a quick pint in the Stag and Fawn in the town. No one in the team was around to ask if they wanted to join him, so he set off alone. Walking the short distance through the streets helped him relax. The pub beckoned with its oak beams, low ceilings, and the hum of casual conversation. Rory just loved the atmosphere. In the winter he also looked forward to the log fire.

As he entered the pub he saw Shaun and Becky at the bar.

'Hi, Rory, just talking about you – the usual?'

'Hi, good I hope. No, just a pint of Steerage, I'm driving, officer,' he replied.

'Yes, actually, we were just saying how cooperation has improved so much over the years and it's proving much more effective when we share information like we do now,' said Shaun.

'Yes, I suppose. I've never known anything else.'

'Oh it didn't used to be like that, I can assure you.'

Moving away from the bar to a quiet table, Rory shared that, 'I've just finished my report on Mr York.' They shared their views on the technicalities of the case and agreed that a tariff of ten to fifteen years was a reasonable expectation.

'We're starting to chase up some of the other players involved, we think we've traced the courier who used to deliver the children to York and are trying to unravel some of the financial implications.

'Accounts of the courier match the profile of one John Chapel, now living in Manchester. However, he's opting to say nothing and it might be difficult to prove. Similarly on the financial side there are some other indications of mismanagement and misappropriation of funds but pinning down who was responsible will no doubt be even more difficult. I also wonder who else knew and tried to cover all this up? As you would expect, there's a whole network of connections here,' said Shaun thoughtfully.

'Do you envisage charging York with fraud too?'

'Maybe, but it could be deemed not to be in the public interest; it wouldn't make any difference to his sentence if the murder charge sticks and he gets life.'

'No, I suppose not,' replied Rory, savouring his pint of Steerage.

Chapter Twenty-Two

The counselling was going well and Rory had one more session before his canal holiday. He had learnt to express some of the negative feelings towards his mother for maintaining the pretence for so long. He was not yet altogether ready to forgive but at least tried to put things in context. The rationale for his natural parents to give him up was entirely understandable, he thought and did not leave him with any residual feelings about rejection. His adopted parents, on balance, he had to acknowledge had done a reasonably good job. He had been loved and cared for during his formative years. It was the deceit that irritated him most, because that was entirely avoidable. That remained a major stumbling block. More food for thought he decided whilst on the boat.

By the time the holiday was due, Rory felt excited. He arrived at the yard early, straight after breakfast and looked at the line of canal boats all waiting for eager passengers. He was shown round and given basic instruction on the operation of the boat and contingencies in the event of any difficulties. It all sounded fairly straightforward. The boat was well equipped, had been recently serviced and had been fully topped up with fuel and water. The man had asked if he had handled a boat before, which of course he hadn't and was then at pains to explain the differences in handling a boat compared to a car. It was obvious really, or at least he thought so. There would be a delay in response to any steering actions and being on moving water meant that stopping wasn't immediate. There were no brakes as such. Slowing or stopping took time and involved the use of reverse gear, therefore concentration and anticipation seemed to be the key.

Rory had a quick test run with the member of staff to ensure that he had understood the basics. Both of them were happy with his performance.

'OK, Mr Scott, the account is paid, you are free to set off, enjoy your trip. You have your route. Customers regularly say that they particularly enjoy that journey through Fradley Junction and turn round near Atherstone locks.'

Rory started to unload the provisions he had bought on the way into the boat, while waiting for Emma, who was late as usual. The boatyard was busy with people checking in and out. There was a repair shed and a little shop, as well as a good fresh food shop and café across the road. It wasn't far from Cannock Chase, twenty square miles of woodland and heath and also close to Shugborough estate managed now entirely by The National Trust. Rory was reading up on canal history. He discovered that Great Haywood was a major canal junction in its day following the completion of the Staffordshire and Worcestershire Canal in 1772 and the Trent and Mersey Canal in 1777. It was the latter that they were due to navigate later.

On Emma's arrival they hugged each other with childlike excitement, finished moving in their luggage and unpacked quickly. Rory had bought some food to cook for dinner and set about finding the heating and lighting controls before they cast the boat off around mid-morning. Tentatively he drove off into the water channel at slow speed before Emma dug him in the ribs, took charge of the controls and confidently manoeuvred the boat through the water building up her speed. Bracken didn't seem quite sure and jumped off onto the bank before it was too late and proceeded to run alongside the boat barking! Emma carefully slowed down to let Rory jump off to join him, just avoiding the temptation to tip him into the water.

They soon both got the basic hang of steering the boat and getting through the locks as they made their way towards Rugeley, where they planned their first night's stop. They travelled through Little Haywood and Colwich, passing under several bridges, counting the numbers down from bridge seventy-three. Travelling over the short aqueduct at Colton was fun! They passed Bishton Hall, now a private school. Opposite used to stand Wolseley Hall but that had become a victim of time and was now a park and craft centre. Children waved as they passed by. Although Rory was familiar with the area he was surprised what a different perspective was revealed from the canal rather than his more regular routes along the road. The pace was of course noticeably different and far more gentle.

As the afternoon unfolded, they decided to moor up against the bank just before they reached Rugeley. After making sure that the boat was secure they congratulated themselves on a pretty successful first day. They put out the folding chairs, opened a bottle of good French wine and sat down to enjoy the view over the fields. Spaghetti Bolognese was cooking slowly on the stove and all looked well with the world.

After a couple of glasses of wine and having caught up on news Emma asked, 'So how are you getting on now with adjusting to your new status, Rory?'

'Oh it's early days yet, Sis, I still feel angry. I don't feel like I can forgive them yet. It's like suddenly having your world turned upside down. All those years of torment, that now it seems could have been avoided.'

PART THREE

Chapter Twenty-Three

Whilst Donald York awaited sentence, DCI Elder was made aware of allegations by two more people who had come forward, claiming to have been abused by York. Both were ex-care residents. One was now living in Shropshire and the other in Scotland. Shaun anticipated that sentencing York would not be delayed any longer but that he could continue to investigate further allegations. It would, after all, be possible to charge York with further offences later. Unravelling the financial and business side of York's affairs was also proving to be difficult and protracted. At this stage Shaun was waiting for an indication from the ACC about the future direction of this whole squalid affair. Shaun knew that the ACC's style was to be thorough, but wondered what resources he would be prepared to commit and for how long to such an investigation?

As he sat down with Becky, Shaun began to review the evidence from the latest complainants. Two statements from two men received within a week of each other. Both were now about the right age for their allegations to be credible and Becky could attempt to verify their connection with Auldbeck from the documents and register that she had already discovered. The statements were similar, amounting to allegations of sexual assault.

'This pattern of behaviour could having been happening for years, don't you think, Sir?' said Becky.

'Yes, quite probably,' Shaun agreed, 'there may be hundreds of victims out there.'

'Frightening isn't it?'

They concluded that it was best at this stage to continue to gather the evidence and then have the option of interviewing York again later. They anticipated that more people would probably continue to come forward. They had seen the tip of the iceberg, you might say.

* * *

Over those summer months, further evidence of York's catalogue of abuse started to become apparent. As publicity increased, more victims started to come forward. For some ex-residents of Auldbeck, abused or not, undoubtedly it was seen as an opportunity to make a quick buck in compensation, but for most it wasn't about money, it was about their suffering being acknowledged. For many of those people their lives had been set on a path of anxiety, depression, sleeplessness and a whole range of personal problems. In the context of the time many felt unable to share their story even with their closest family and friends, effectively sentencing themselves to fear, loneliness and isolation. When the story became public and they started to realise that they were not alone, that in itself was some comfort. Then the sheer relief of feeling free to openly describe those events to a third party, was for many so powerful in helping to release their great burden of secrecy. Some felt a strong desire to see their suffering result in those responsible being held to account. For some it was more about preventing any further abuse and for others the prospect of the exposure and consequent legal process held nothing but fear and dread of being reminded of a traumatic experience that they had hoped to forget.

As news of another public sex abuse scandal broke, the inevitable outcry began. Shock and moral indignation followed. Subsequently there were demands for an enquiry, which over time began to gain momentum. For the police there would be difficult decisions ahead about how many resources to commit to an ongoing investigation. At this stage at least a sufficient case had been made to bring York to court with the prospect of a substantial sentence. Further actions could follow and evidence be added to the growing state of awareness about the frightening level of prevalence of sexual abuse.

92

Chapter Twenty-Four

Morning had arrived on the barge with the prospect of a warm sunny day to come. Emma looked out over the fields, enjoying the typical English view of cows in the field, church spires and hawthorn hedgerows. Bracken looked up at her as if to say yes and there are so many sniffs too! He looked for permission as he pondered jumping off the boat to explore the towpath. Emma nodded and he was gone like a rocket into the hedgerow and far beyond. She watched with pleasure as he ran free across the open ground with his tail fanning him forward. Rory was making himself busy in the galley. It had to be bacon and eggs, he considered, having brought fresh eggs with him from a farm near where he lived and bacon from a traditional butcher. He glanced up momentarily towards Emma and felt a warmth and comfort in just being with her. It had been so kind of her to suggest and organise the trip, he thought. He joined her on the deck and looked out over the fields.

'Is that Bracken over there in the brambles? What has he got in his mouth?' enquired Rory.

'I can't really see from here,' replied Emma as she turned to him. 'He is a lovely dog isn't he?'

'Yep, sure is,' Rory responded.

'You know what, I really fancy bacon and eggs,' announced Emma as Bracken bounded back onto the boat with a rabbit in his mouth.

'It looks like Bracken has other ideas for his breakfast!'

Breakfast lived up to expectations and Rory skinned and gutted the rabbit to make a casserole for dinner, not forgetting to leave some for his efficient hunter.

'So where are we heading for today, Rory?' Emma enquired.

'Well, it's on to Fradley junction near Lichfield, staying on the Trent and Mersey Canal, next to the A38 heading to Burton,' he responded. 'Fancy a pub lunch?'

'Um, sounds good to me!' Emma responded looking forward to the possibility.

She let Rory drive the first section while she cleared up the breakfast things thinking that they really did get on awfully well. The boat glided through the water at a reassuringly leisurely pace onwards under another series of bridges. Getting the hang of passing under the bridges seemed OK but the locks were obviously more of a challenge for novices; mooring the boat, managing the lock water flow, driving in and out, are all an acquired skill. Early days brought their fair share of minor bumps as they progressed through the narrow channels. They realised that they would need to have their skills refined before reaching the locks at Fradley Junction.

'How are you feeling about dad and all of that now, Rory?' Emma enquired gently as they meandered forward through the water.

'You mean the revelation that he wasn't my dad and me being adopted and all that?' he replied.

'Yes, you poor thing,' she responded sympathetically.

'It's still very raw, sis.'

'Yes I'm sure, but in a way it's a relief isn't it?'

'What in the sense that I never felt fully part of the family, as you did? Yes I suppose so, but having answered that question it begs a series of others, sis. I keep coming back to who actually am I?'

'Oh dear, you are you, don't beat yourself up about it,' said Emma trying to be reassuring.

'Easier said than done, Emma. I know now that my father wasn't actually my father but then who was? Mum hasn't given me many clues.'

'But does it matter?' posed Emma in her usual matter-of-fact way.

'Well yes, of course it does. I want to know my family background,' he responded, feeling slightly hurt.

'Well you'll just have to find out then, won't you?' Emma declared.

Rory opted to walk along the canal bank with Bracken,

wishing that he saw things in such black and white terms as his sister, but the fact was that he didn't. He felt in turmoil. Bracken ran along the bank sniffing and foraging, helping to restore a sense of normality. Rory tried to move on in his mind and think of the here and now as he picked up a stick and threw it for Bracken. The sunlight shone across the fields and the warmth of the day was a pleasant change from the stuffy atmosphere of the office. As he walked round the bend with Emma following on dutifully in the boat she shouted out to him.

'Hey, Rory, that looks like the pub ahead and it's my round!'

* * *

Shaun was reviewing developments in the York case with Becky. A date had been set for sentencing at Stafford Crown Court. That usually gave the victims some sense of relief if not justice, they both thought.

'The financial side of the enquiry is dragging now, Sir, as we anticipated that it would. Trying to uncover historical evidence is slow work,' reported Becky.

'Then we shall be patient,' responded Shaun. 'Any more witnesses or potential victims come forward yet?'

'No more as of yesterday. Oh, the two latest respondents' names don't appear on any of the rolls we have from Auldbeck,' she remembered.

'OK, but they aren't likely to be entirely complete records, are they Becky?'

'No, I doubt it, Sir,' she responded.

'Potential gold diggers then, Becky?'

'Could be, Sir.'

* * *

The Ash Tree pub at Armitage sat on the waterfront by the canal with ample room to pull in and secure the boat. Emma steered her in confidently while Rory quickly leapt off stumbling before securing the ropes.

'Shall we sit outside?' Emma asked, anticipating agreement. 'I'll go and order some drinks and fetch a menu. Look there's a water bowl there for Bracken!'

'OK, sis, a pint of… oh you know what I like,' he concurred.

While Bracken had a drink from the dog bowl, Rory selected a table with a good view back across the canal. Children were happily playing, giving their parents a welcome break. He sat down reflecting how pleased he was to have his sister's support. Emma soon arrived with the drinks and a menu.

'Lovely, so what's that?' he enquired looking longingly at the pint.

'Try it and guess. It's a guest ale,' said Emma, laying down the challenge.

'Um, a light ale, is it local?'

'Yes, Slater's brewery.'

'Then it's got to be Top Totty hasn't it?'

'Correct,' Emma declared as they both laughed.

Rory decided on the beef and ale pie while Emma selected a Cajun chicken salad. Lunch soon arrived and was well received. Good company, a relaxing drink and nice food all helped to generate a sense of escape from the rigours of their normal busy lives with the prospect of reflection about their new-found circumstances.

After just sitting enjoying the fresh air accompanied by another drink, it was time to move on. They chugged on past The Crown at Hansacre and arrived at the planned destination of Fradley Junction by early evening, in time for tea and cakes. They had decided to eat in tonight, following the generous pub lunch. But before any further thoughts of food, they first set off to explore with Bracken.

Walking new sections of the towpath was always revealing with new perspectives, views and places of interest. There was also an attraction in meeting new people. Towpaths were a wealth of richness in their experience with people offering local information, advice on looking after dogs and opinions on everything from the weather to high politics. Today was no different as they met and started talking to a couple who had taken early retirement and bought a boat. Their story was fascinating; from fitting the boat out themselves to selling their house and breaking free from conventional living. They had toured extensively through the English and Welsh canal network and were just embarking on a tour of some of their favourite routes.

The following day the weather had turned wet, Emma had decided that it was Rory's turn to steer the boat as they embarked on the next leg of the journey towards Tamworth. There would be no pub lunch today, it was head down and steam on to the next stopping point. The poor weather restricted the views but failed to temper Bracken's enthusiasm. They chugged on under several bridges, onto The Coventry Canal and past Lichfield, then past Whittington and Hopwas towards their target destination.

As the rain dripped down his collar, Rory couldn't avoid thoughts and feelings of unease racing through his mind. Memories returned of occasions and events that, looking back on it, could have been different. He thought of family parties, holidays and Christmas when conversations reflected assumptions and views that he felt uncomfortable with. He could never understand why at the time, but now it was evident. He remembered being punished by his father as a child for some trivial misdemeanour. How his dad had been so irate and the more that Rory tried to explain that he didn't think it was important, the more his father became exasperated with his errant child. All those missed connections, all those misunderstandings.

As they approached Tamworth with its castle, Emma joined Rory outside to see them through to the mooring point.

'What do you fancy later, sis?' he asked. 'A walk into town and a curry?'

'Yes, Rory, that sounds fine. No Vindaloo for you though – remember we sleep in a confined space!'

After finding a place to moor up, they left the boat to follow the path into town. Bracken confidently led the way as if this was familiar territory. A signpost soon indicated a path into the town and they strolled happily along taking in the scenery. Once into the town they walked along its urban streets, looking out for possible venues before spying a Wetherspoon's pub.

'That will do for me!' announced Emma with certainty and Bracken seemed to agree by pulling on his lead. They sat down to settle Bracken before Emma went to the bar to review the range of beers for Rory. She generally drank lager or gin and tonic but liked to view the beer range with their colourful images and often wacky names. It may not have been terribly scientific but she usually selected the most bizarre combination of name and label. She supposed it was partly familiarity with advertising and her commercial background. Today her eye was caught by a Robinson's bitter called Trooper. She returned to the table with Rory's beer and her lager to find that he had cheated again by observing her selection and denying her the opportunity to invite him to profess his comprehensive knowledge and attempt to identify the beer blind. She glanced at him with disapproval.

'So, what are you going to do next, Rory, to cast light on your family background?' Emma asked.

'Um, I suppose my first port of call will be Social Services to access the records, then go from there,' he replied.

'OK. You realise don't you that your new family may not be all that you want it to be?' Emma posed with caution.

'What do you mean?'

'Well they might be wholesome hard-working folks with endearing characteristics, but equally they may all be mass murders?' she said trying to inject some realism into her brother's thinking.

'Yes, but without asking I'll never know will I? If you're warning against unrealistic expectations then fair enough, or if you're asking how far am I prepared to go with this, then I simply don't know at this stage. I am sure, however, that I want to take the first steps and see where that leads me.'

Emma sensed his slight irritation and left it at that for now, just hoping that he didn't end up being disappointed.

'Another drink? Shall I choose? But no cheating this time; you must try to guess what it is… there's quite a range.'

'Yes, surprise me!' Rory replied eagerly, placing his hands over his face and trying to look through his fingers like a child.

'What is it then?' he asked on her return.

'No, you try it then guess,' she said impishly.

'Um, a nice sharp bitter; we are close to Burton, so Burton Bridge?'

'You must have looked, you cheated again!' challenged Emma, slapping his thigh and chuckling. He loved it when she was like that.

The curry proved to be a hit. Bracken had to stay outside, but they could see him through the window. They saved him a few crumbs of papadom to reward his patience. They walked back arm-in-arm, only disturbed by Rory's diversions into the hedge before getting back to the boat.

At the start of day four it was time to review the original plan. Was it too ambitious to head for Atherstone locks, with fourteen locks to encounter before turning round? They concluded that it probably was and decided to be pragmatic and settle for Fazeley Junction then turn round via the junction with the Birmingham and Fazeley Canal and return towards Lichfield before stopping overnight. That would allow for two long days and a return back to Haywood by the end of day six which suited them both.

Their decision proved to be sensible, they thought, as

they enjoyed the views whilst passing over the Tame Aqueduct. They realised that they were not far from Drayton Manor Park, but resisted the temptation to divert. Maybe next time, they thought.

They followed their planned route, continuing to enjoy each other's company and to explore Rory's feelings about his change of status. He was now aware of something about his parents but wanted to know more about them and about his extended family and grandparents; some longer term sense of who he was and where he had come from. Rory tried to see this as exciting rather than threatening but despite his best efforts he felt that it was probably both feelings intertwined. What character traits that he had believed were at odds with his family were actually in tune, he wondered? What values were grounded in generations of tradition? He longed to feel a part of something beyond being an individual, some sense of belonging and of destiny.

Emma steered the boat confidently onwards towards Lichfield. It was quite breezy but still pleasant. Rory was walking alongside the boat with Bracken. Emma thought that it looked like Bracken could jump across at any moment so she pulled out a little more into the centre of the waterway, whilst making sure to look out for other boats coming the other way. They made good progress and passed under several bridges before they began to approach Whittington.

Rory and Bracken returned onto the boat and Rory took his turn at driving the last section. They decided to stop overnight at Whittington and eat in The Dog pub in the village. Rory managed to steer successfully to a suitable mooring. They secured the boat and put out the camping chairs on the towpath to enjoy surveying the scenery. Emma started to laugh. Turning towards her brother she said, 'Rory, do you remember that time when dad had gone to some trouble to find you a holiday job with one of his friends who ran an accountancy firm?'

'Oh yes,' he replied, starting to smile. 'He came home

all excited to tell me that it was all arranged and that I could start the following day. He had worked out travel details, made sure with mum that I had suitable clothes to wear, anticipated paying me a lunch allowance… all that, but never thought to ask me if I was interested.'

'Yes, that's right. Then when you simply said that it was kind of him but that you had other plans, he blew a fuse and got really angry with you, didn't he?' Emma remembered.

'Yes and then attempted to lecture me about being ungrateful!'

* * *

Meanwhile Becky's enquiries were beginning to unravel some interesting connections. After diligently searching through records retrieved from York's house and further information extracted from the bank, she felt that she was making some progress. It was time to report back to Shaun and she knew that her DCI would be interested.

'Hi, Becky, everything OK?' Shaun asked as he breezed past her back at the police station.

'Actually, Sir, I could do with a word,' she replied hopefully.

'OK, my office in half an hour. I'll see you then.'

Becky felt relieved. That gave her a chance to consider her findings and be able to present her concerns. She hoped to secure some guidance about what to do next. The half-hour soon passed as she bundled up her papers and went to report to her DCI.

She knocked at the door, he beckoned and she walked confidently into the office and sat down.

'So, what have you found, Becky?'

'Well, Sir, the financial records from Auldbeck aren't complete and entries and payments are mostly for small amounts from a wide variety of sources,' she paused and took a deep breath. 'However, there is one consistent thread.'

'Go on,' invited Shaun, eager to hear what his able colleague had found.

'There are different names used but the account numbers tally. In addition to the money York took for himself from the radio station, I'd say about another twenty per cent of the money received by Auldbeck from charitable donations was effectively hived off too.'

'OK, is it possible to say to where or by whom?' Shaun enquired.

'Not with sufficient certainty to convince a court yet, Sir, but some of that money was transferred before Auldbeck closed into an account which still exists,' Becky replied.

* * *

The following day on the boat demanded an early start to allow sufficient time to reach Hansacre and the sanctuary of The Crown pub for dinner. That would be the next overnight stop. Their plan worked out well, leaving their last day to return back to Great Haywood and the boatyard.

They woke early, eager to embark on the last leg of their journey. They decided to skip breakfast and just crack on, anticipating no time for a last pub lunch. Indeed, they found that they did need to just keep going, so Emma made some sandwiches while Rory steered the boat. They began to realise that they had been very ambitious in their planning, expecting to cover the distances set easily, but it was too late now and they just needed to crack on without stopping. After enjoying the views, with sandwich in hand Rory stepped onto the bank again to walk with Bracken while Emma took over. They found that they could easily exchange roles with the minimum of fuss, feeling very relaxed in each other's company, overriding any feelings of discomfort about being rushed through their less than perfect planning.

A last walk and final reflections allowed Rory to continue thinking about his new circumstances. Whilst some questions had been answered, some remained but he felt OK about that; he'd made reasonable progress. He was trying not to think about work and just to enjoy the last part of the journey. He knew that he was going to miss his sister's company

They arrived back at the boatyard in the early evening, just in time before the last member of staff left and were relieved to be able to hand the boat over quickly. It had been a great experience and they thanked the staff for their help and advice before going their separate ways. Best to keep the goodbyes short, they both felt.

Chapter Twenty-Five

By the day of the trial, the memory of the canal holiday already seemed an age away. Rory felt that he hadn't had a minute to himself since returning to work. Reports, actions on cases, not to mention supporting his mother had all been demanding his attention. Donald York was due to be sentenced at Stafford Crown Court that morning, having pleaded guilty to all counts. All the indications were that the sentence would be substantial. Rory checked his report again and tried to anticipate any gaps or questions that the Judge may ask.

As he entered the court building and passed through security it was evident that the case was going to attract considerable interest. Members of the police team, witnesses, victims and their families and the press all stood waiting for proceedings to start. He exchanged a brief glance and nod with Becky and Shaun as they took their places.

The court fell silent as Donald York was led into the dock and the Judge took up his seat. The usual formalities took place with York confirming his name and address before the Judge made his statement and announced sentence. Finally, a reduced charge of manslaughter relating to the death of Molly Bennett had been secured, given some doubt about how far her death was due to her asthma as against solely his actions. Additional charges were also listed as four counts of sexual assault and one of theft of charitable funds to the value of a notional £5,000. Manslaughter could be subject to a discretionary, as against mandatory, life sentence so the important details of his sentencing were in the hands of the Judge as the court awaited his address. He cleared his throat and began his pronouncement.

'Donald York, you were a trusted celebrity with a considerable following. You deliberately used your fame to gain access to children knowing that your intention was to abuse them. You constructed a process of abuse that you continued over a long period of time, harming some of the most vulnerable members of our community. You went on to use your influence to subdue any protests or suspicions that arose over those years.

'One of your victims also died in the course of your abuse. Her brother has suffered torment over all those years since her disappearance, for which you have expressed not a scrap of regret or remorse save for the likely impact on yourself. You also abused your position of trust in the financial dealing of the charity concerned, seeking to make money from other people's misery and used funds donated for charitable good for your own purposes.

'I commend both the medical and probation report writers who have assisted me in my deliberations, and both independently have drawn the conclusion that you continue to represent a high risk to children. It is my duty to protect the public from serious offenders such as you.

'Donald York, for the offence of manslaughter, I exercise my discretion and sentence you to life imprisonment with a minimum tariff of fifteen years. For the offences of sexual assault I sentence you to two years on each count and three years for the offence of theft, all to be served concurrently. You will be subject to sex offender registration for life with a number of restrictions designed to assist the authorities in monitoring your progress and alert them to any indications of future inappropriate behaviour. Take him down.'

As York was led away with no indication of any reaction, the court was filled with relief, tears and shouts from the public gallery that he should never be released. Victims attempted to comfort each other, knowing that this was a major milestone in their journeys but not the end. Professionals began to walk away with some sense of achievement and the Judge returned to his chambers hoping that he had done his duty and got the sentencing balance right.

Rory walked back to his car and returned to the office. There was usually a sense of anti-climax after the conclusion of a big case like this and he felt drained. He knew that the court staff would interview York before he was taken to a local prison for initial allocation, as against the remand prison where he had been held. That could be one of several moves before being allocated to a prison best suited to deal with him. He knew that he would need to visit York and work with the prison staff to help construct a sentence plan, but that could wait for now. Today he needed a coffee and then to get on with catching up with his other work. He was pleased that the Judge had set a life sentence and a substantial tariff as that secured much greater control over York's future than a determinate sentence of a fixed number of years. In order to secure eventual release, if at all, York would have to satisfy the Parole Board that his risk had been sufficiently reduced to make him manageable in the community. He anticipated that he may struggle to achieve that, at least on current evidence. Rory expected a period of anger and acting out 'poor me' before any real willingness to look at the harm that he had caused. If Rory was proved to be right, as a convicted sex offender York was not likely to start any meaningful work for several years.

* * *

Shaun and Becky also returned to their office base. Their journey back being completed in near silence. Both felt exhausted after the months of preparation to get to this point. For them securing the safe confinement of such a dangerous man was almost cause for celebration. Shaun would need to address his team and thank them before some of them were stood down and reassigned to other duties. In that sense he was almost sad to reach the end, as he had created a good team and would miss them, but he knew that he had to move on. The ACC was pleased, so that was something.

However, before losing the momentum the police would need to decide whether to continue with the wider financial investigations or accept that the evidence was difficult to retrieve and that the chances of further prosecution too limited to justify any more resources. Decisions would also need to be made about whether to charge York with any further counts of sexual assault as new evidence emerged. Shaun remained sceptical, however, about the validity of the accusations from the last two men to come forward. Their statements seemed too contrived and almost identical. It could not be established whether or not they had actually resided at Auldbeck at all. It could be a case of two ex-care residents seeing the publicity and deciding to make a complaint, hoping for substantial compensation. Sadly that was not uncommon, Shaun reflected. He would need to interview the two men again and they could be charged with perverting the course of justice if he felt that they were simply on the make.

Either way, Shaun and Becky were still hopeful about bringing a case against Gerald Ross, the care home manager at the time, for assisting and abetting the abuse of children. There was also Becky's research to complete in unravelling further financial misdemeanours. Ross had proved to be very resistant to 'helping the police with their enquiries'. It was times like this that they were reminded that offences once committed could still be investigated many years later. The message was a sound one in both public reassurance and deterrence.

Chapter Twenty-Six

Several long talks with his sister whilst navigating the canals had helped Rory decide his next step. Despite the risks, he did want to contact Social Services with a view to finding out more about his real family background.

Initial consultation laid out the process, which seemed fairly straightforward. There was no requirement for prior counselling, but the Social Worker might intervene if the records were particularly difficult or harrowing. Rory received an indication that in his case the records were not unduly complicated. Eventually, after some inevitable processing, including verifying his official identity, Rory was invited to view an edited version of his original adoption file.

On the day, he was feeling both excited and mildly anxious. He was greeted at the records office by a stern-looking lady, he guessed in her late sixties and led to a dusty old file and a quiet place in which to read it. The member of staff said that she was on hand if required. Rory took a deep breath and opened the file to find brief but enlightening information. He flicked through the pages to find a 'later in life letter' from the Social Worker at the time and handwritten notes from each of his parents directly to him. There were also some photographs of them and Rory felt a warm connection and a resemblance to particularly his mother. As he had been led to believe, his parents had met at university and conceived a child unexpectedly and out of wedlock. Neither of them saw themselves as ready to become parents, so with some sadness and mixed feelings had bowed to the pressure of the time to give up their child for adoption, in preference to seeking an abortion. He also learnt that both his parents were the first generation in their family to go to university. They were both studying law at the time, which interesting he thought given his own connection to criminal justice. Rory felt satisfied with the information and felt no burning desire to try to trace them or to meet them at this stage or to take copies of what he had read. He did take a few notes, however. His concentration was still on tracing his family tree back through the generations and getting a sense of his roots. He sat at the desk for a moment with a quiet tear before thanking the staff and leaving the building to return to the office.

So his mother had been right that his natural parents were two students who had a relationship at university and were persuaded to give up their baby for adoption. His father was indeed a Mr Carpenter and his mother a Miss Tiller. Details about them, however, were sketchy.

Armed with what little information there was in official records, Rory started to set about the task of constructing a family history; a genealogy. He needed some luck to get started. Emma had mentioned their mother's revelation to some members of the family and had received a mixed reaction. Some of them appeared to think that the secret should have remained concealed and that no good would come from its exposure as a lie. However, one aunt took a different view – Aunt Grace had struggled with a dilemma for many years. She wasn't aware of the whole picture but had her doubts about the family's claim of a miracle birth of a second child when Rory's mother had already told her herself that she couldn't have any more children after Emma.

Having reflected on it, she eventually decided to contact Rory direct and break her silence. When Rory received her letter it was most unexpected. She expressed her concern and her regret that the truth had emerged in such circumstances and wrote about her own misgivings about the family. She also mentioned that she had heard that Mr Carpenter's grandfather – Rory's great-grandfather – had left for Australia in the early part of the twentieth century. Maybe this was the break that he had hoped for? It seemed like a useful starting point, to chase up any trace in Australia. Initially, Rory had sought information from Somerset House and the local William Salt Library in

Stafford. It was only when he started to make enquires that he realised that most of these historical records were now available to all online. The library did, nevertheless, provide some useful background history and context about the development of the canal network across Staffordshire. Rory discovered that Mr Carpenter's father was from a working-class background and had lived in Shropshire. He made lock gates for the canals.

After further research, Rory did manage to find records of Mr Carpenter's family tree, but there were gaps. The family were all craftsmen it seemed with a long history of working on the canal network. His great-grandfather didn't seem to fit the general trend, however. He needed to dig a little further.

Through a friend in Australia, Rory started to try to trace Samuel Zacharias Carpenter his great-grandfather. Immigration records in Australia proved to be quite comprehensive but after trawling through ledgers from 1900 to 1920, no match could be found. The picture seemed confusing.

Chapter Twenty-Seven

Several months were to pass by. Rory engaged in careful research. He started to piece together information from different sources. This of course had to be fitted in around work, supporting his mother and looking after Bracken. His mother was not coping well with her new circumstances. Rory and his sister were spending a good deal of time trying to support her.

Rory tried hard to use his counselling sessions to address his own concerns and anxieties. The counsellor was good at reflecting back, encouraging him to express his feelings and challenging him to think through his responses. Over time she helped him let go of most of the negative feelings towards his mother, he accepted that these were not productive. She had done what she thought was right at the time, without malice. He didn't agree with her but that was OK. Better to concentrate on his fact finding and to channel his energies into uncovering some truths. This helped him see the journey as more of an opportunity than a threat and actually something quite exciting He was encouraged to learn from his sister's matter-of-fact approach and try not to agonise too much. He found that the very act of meeting regularly, having designated time and expressing his thoughts to a neutral listener were all therapeutic.

Meanwhile, Donald York had been processed through prison allocation initially to a category A jail in the north of England. HMP Southgate was an old-style prison based on an ex-military garrison. Extensions over the years had added new facilities but the castle-like facade remained.

Category A was the highest level of security where most life sentence prisoners would start serving their term. Prisoner movement was highly restricted and behaviour and attitude closely monitored. As a child sex offender, York was placed in the vulnerable prisoners unit for his own protection. A necessary provision to maintain good order and discipline but concentrating the most difficult, entrenched and dangerous sex offenders together had the potential to undermine any positive progress that the authorities could hope to make. Sharing their experiences with each all tended to give such prisoners opportunities to reinforce their own mindset of self-justification. They were living day to day, mostly with other serious sex offenders who tended to see nothing wrong with their behaviour and therefore confirmed rather than challenged their distorted view of the world. The task of the authorities was to break this complacency through individual work with psychology and through sex offender treatment programmes.

Rory was due to visit. He booked with the prison well in advance. Allowing for the journey and the security restrictions in gaining access to the prison he anticipated a full day commitment. After a brisk walk with Bracken he set off towards Uttoxeter for the A50 and access to the M1 north. Journeys were a rare opportunity to think and to plan what he hoped to achieve in the day. Rory anticipated resistance and even hostility. He didn't expect compliance and cooperation. Throughout his contact with this case, Donald York had sought to down play his activities and concentrate on his own felt needs and wanted to avoid any consideration of the consequences for others, particularly his victims. Whilst this was not unusual, it was unhelpful and needed to be challenged through the long journey of breaking down the layers of twisted thinking and presenting York with the realities of the harm he had done.

Rory approached the prison, found the car park and set off towards the main gate armed with his ID card, plus pen and paper, having left everything else in the car to avoid complications later. The security checks were rigorous with a metal detector, body search and detailed questioning before he was allowed through and into the visits hall. He reported in again and was checked off on their list and invited to sit at table number seven and wait for York to be escorted to him. York had not been placed on closed visits where conversation was conducted through a glass screen to avoid any direct contact and chance of smuggling in contraband. Visitors were regularly pressurised or bullied into attempting to smuggle in particularly drugs or mobile phone parts. Obviously, Rory was aware of that and had no intention of falling foul of the process; it would be unprofessional and more than his job was worth. He remained surprised, nonetheless, that some staff in prisons did try to bring things in for prisoners. He had asked the officer in charge if he could also find a member of the prison offender management team to meet him to discuss the sentence plan.

An officer from offender management arrived promptly and shared her perceptions. Donald York had been very guarded in what he had shared with staff and was still very much licking his wounds. A process that the prison was used to and was happy to let him wallow, allowing more time for those prisoners who wanted to engage. Managing a life sentence was a lengthy process and simply allowing a prisoner 'to do their time' for the first few years could be part of that journey. Targets for sentence planning therefore were modest at this stage. He would wait to be allocated to a psychologist to start exploring the nature of his offences. In the meantime, there was prison work and day-to-day activity. He had been allocated to a light industrial shop, packing toilet rolls into boxes.

The officer had to leave before York arrived.

'Mr York for you, Sir,' announced the escort as the prisoner sat down.

'Donald, how are you? I'm Rory Scot, your Probation Officer, remember me? I wrote your report for court.'

'Yes and what a pack of lies that was!' came the curt reply.

Rory obviously didn't agree, but chose not to react straight away. 'How are you adjusting and settling in?' asked Rory.

'Settling in! It's not some form of fucking hotel you know – you don't settle into a place like this. I'm wearing clothes other prisoners have worn. I'm told what to do, when to eat and the food is diabolical!' York replied indignantly.

York was already attracting the attention of the supervising staff and was warned about his conduct.

'Look, I've travelled some distance to come to see you today but I can leave now and record that you failed to cooperate or we can use the time as constructively as possible. Which is it to be?' responded Rory assertively.

'Constructive! What's constructive about being banged up in some medieval fort?'

'The reality is you have been sentenced to life and this is only just the beginning of the process. I can try to help you adjust and give you some idea of how your sentence may be managed.'

'Do you really think I need reminding? I'd rather they hanged me,' York replied, starting to get emotional and putting his head in his hands.

'Do you think you deserve that?'

'No, of course not! I've done nothing wrong,' York responded adamantly.

'Donald, the case against you was solid. You severely damaged many children who were already traumatised.'

'Oh don't give me that shit. They weren't real children. They were runaways. Nobodies. No one cared. They had no future anyway. They were already messed up by the time I got involved. I couldn't have made it any worse for them,' York said trying desperately to justify his actions.

'But you did, Donald, you did,' Rory concluded.

Chapter Twenty-Eight

'Mr Chas' soon found that his celebrity status didn't count for much in prison. Even amongst sex offenders some of the other prisoners on the wing simply looked straight through him with total disdain and ignored him completely. Others were more vocal in their condemnation. He was starting to feel isolated and somewhat lonely, as well as totally dejected. The reaction of his family and friends had varied from total rejection to tacit support. His wife had initially promised to stand by him but the pressure of the trial and family influence had proved to be too much and she had filed for divorce. She had moved away to her sister's after feeling hounded out of her house. His two children had been deeply hurt and very upset. After which one chose to support him, believing his cries of innocence and the other condemned him out of hand. The public and press reaction had been highly critical of York's abusive pattern of behaviour and of a system that allowed it to go on for so long. It raised difficult questions again of power and celebrity.

The growing realisation was dawning that he was no longer going to be able to bluff, bully and buy his way out of this one. For him the very thought was devastating. Out there he had been important. Now he was nothing, just another prisoner amongst many. He tried to contact outside, but most people didn't reply to his letters. For the first time that he could remember, Donald York was beginning to feel lonely in such a crowded place. He had written to his solicitor demanding an immediate return to court for reconsideration but had only received a curt reply stating that there were no grounds to pursue an appeal. This was all new to him; Donald York was discovering what it was like to be insignificant, miserable, alone, exposed and rejected.

Prison life was slow, dominated by routine and endless security considerations. One day 'Mr Chas' was riding high in the public's regard and the next he had been arrested and remanded in custody. He had never gone back to his house or had any idea what had happened to his possessions. Seemingly in an instant his world of power, celebrity and sexual exploitation had been shattered. He could see nothing ahead of him but despair.

'Ryan wants to see you, Boss,' said one of the officers to the wing manager.

'OK, wheel him in.'

'Morning, I have some news for you.'

'Just shut the door then,' cautioned the officer.

'Some of these low lives have hatched a plot to mark York. Mangeli has a razor blade attached to a toothbrush and they plan to cut his face tomorrow,' reported Michael Ryan, ex-police officer, dispassionately.

'OK, you sure, Ryan?'

'Well I haven't just made it up for fun,' he replied sarcastically.

'So what do you want me to do?'

'Clear the wing and let them do it properly as far as I'm concerned, but if I were you I'd order an immediate cell search.'

'OK. On your way,' said the wing manager returning to his crossword.

'Jones,' he shouted to the wing orderly, 'more tea!'

Sure enough, the cell search revealed a weapon as Ryan had described. Mangeli was taken down to the block and there were some very disappointed prisoners left on the wing with only one question. Who had grassed them up?

Michael Ryan was a police officer who had been unfortunate enough to be caught by professional standards officers with his fingers in the till. He was taking bribes to protect a drug gang in Manchester and one of his colleagues had noticed his sudden and dramatic increase in fortune and spending power and had reported it. Breach of trust and abuse of public office are taken very seriously and Ryan had ended up with an eight-year sentence and had been dismissed from the force. As an ex-copper he was an immediate target in the prison with prisoners queuing up to have a go at one of 'them'. For his own protection he had been advised that realistically he needed to spend the whole of his sentence in vulnerable prisoner units. Hence his inclusion in this murky wing of sex offenders, the vulnerable and other disgraced officials.

Two days later, the manager called for Ryan.

'Ryan, come in, close the door. We're hearing that other prisoners were mightily pissed off at the discovery of the weapon and have asked themselves who split on them. The number one candidate is you, for obvious reasons. I'm just warning you, can you deal with that?' posed the wing manager

'If you think I'm going to be intimidated by the likes of these misfits and creatures then forget it. I'll stand my ground and happily break the neck of any of the bastards who try it on with me,' responded Ryan forthrightly.

'OK, well that's one way of dealing with it, but just be careful, that's all I'm saying.'

'OK, Boss, and I'd do the same again. I'm still a copper at heart,' said Ryan calmly as he left and stared out the eyes that observed him leaving the office.

Chapter Twenty-Nine

Rory had to conclude that he had drawn a blank as regards any link with Australia. There was no record of a Samuel Zacharias Carpenter having emigrated from England around that time. Rory was also confused by further information that emerged about the family thereafter. Local newspaper stories from the time indicated that Sam was a heavy drinker and an unreliable worker, often reported to have spent the night in police cells. It seemed fair to conclude that the family with their four children would have struggled. When Rory received the death certificate he had sent for relating to his great-grandmother, it only added to his uncertainty and quest for the truth. She had died in 1918 from influenza, leaving Sam with the four children. Again newspaper reports of her death were quickly followed by the story of his imprisonment for assaulting the local constable and the four children being taken away by Barnardos. More research and requests for birth and death certificates revealed the fate of the four children. One died soon after her mother. One was sent to Canada to work on a farm and was subsequently killed in the Second World War, and the remaining two boys were adopted in the UK.

After months of painstaking effort, eventually Rory did manage to trace Mrs Mandy Browning, the granddaughter of one of those two boys freed up for adoption. She was married and lived in Bath with her own family. After some correspondence and several phone calls, Rory secured agreement to meet on neutral ground in Worcester.

As he set off to meet his distant relative, Rory felt a mixture of emotions. He wasn't seeking a sustained relationship with this new-found member of his family, just some insight into his history. What would she look like? Would there be a resemblance, he wondered?

Rory parked in Worcester in good time, remembering how Emma had tried to lower his expectations and keep him grounded. After all nothing might come of the meeting.

They had arranged to meet in a churchyard in the city centre. He stood feeling self-conscious by a large tree and waited. Time passed slowly as the meeting time approached, arrived and passed. Then just as he wondered whether she'd had second thoughts, a woman approached slowly from the opposite side of the churchyard. As she got nearer, Rory felt himself becoming emotional. It was obvious that they shared a certain likeness. When she stopped in front of him neither of them could speak but just held each other in their arms whilst they shared a tear.

After embarrassed introductions followed by laughter, they set off to find a cafe. She started to tell her grandmother's story. She repeated to Rory what her grandmother had told her over the years; that her adopted family had done a good job and that she never felt the need to trace her own family and had just got on with her life. Contact from Rory had been a surprise, a shock even. Rory was quick to apologise but she reassured him that there was no need. He tried to press her on any memories that she may have had about her grandmother's early life. She began to cry again as she recalled the stories of shouting, the fights and the drunkenness. She obviously had no love for her great-grandfather and pitied her poor mother. She remembered her mother crying many times about her first husband, who she was told had emigrated to Australia. She was adamant that he would never have done that willingly and missed him desperately. In order to protect her three children she had remarried in haste and had always regretted it.

Rory listened intently, trying to take it all in. He held her hand as she continued: 'Your grandfather was the fourth child and his mother loved him so much. He was born soon after her second marriage when everything changed. After that I remember my grandmother telling me that her mother had had two miscarriages due to our great-grandfather's drunken rages. I didn't think about it as a child but over the years I have wondered whether her love for your grandfather was as a connection back to her first husband.'

'You mean that she was already pregnant before she remarried?' asked Rory for confirmation.

'Yes, love, I do,' she replied.

'Do you remember her first husband's name?'

'Yes, he was George Tiller.'

* * *

Shaun was busy sending all the necessary evidence to his colleagues out of area to be able to arrest Gerald Ross for a variety of charges in relation to being complicit in the trafficking and abuse of children in his care, whilst he was the manager of Auldbeck.

He was diligent in this regard, being very careful from bitter experience not to leave any procedural gaps for some smart-arse lawyer to exploit and secure his release. Shaun wanted to see Ross charged and held in custody before the day was out.

Becky was still working on building a case against other members of staff but that was proving to be more difficult. Some had since died, others were in very poor health and the evidence trail was weakening.

The CPS considered whether or not it was in the public interest to bring further charges against Donald York. Realistically it would be unlikely to result in extending his term in custody or play a significant part in any future considerations about potential release. Nevertheless, sometimes despite that, the interests of justice particularly for the victims was an overriding consideration. However, Shaun was not optimistic given the strains on the system that this was going to be perceived as a priority.

There was also a report waiting for Shaun from HMP Southgate of an incident involving York where one of the other prisoners had assaulted him. Notions of relative moral hierarchy were an odd feature of prison life, Shaun thought. Offenders in general saw certain categories of their number as lesser beings. The lowest of the low were those who attacked elderly people, child sex offenders and baby killers. As such York was a clear candidate for internal judgement and retribution from mere rapists and pimps. His injuries were relatively minor however, resulting from an assisted slip in the showers and seemed destined to be dealt with by internal prison disciplinary procedures and not require the attention of the police.

The prison internal investigation had concluded that given the level of animosity expressed towards York by other prisoners, despite their best efforts to prevent it, a successful assault was inevitable at some point. Intelligence suggested that Idris Jones was the instigator. He was serving four years for rape and had always insisted that sex was consensual with the girl in question and it only transpired afterwards that she was in fact only sixteen years old. As such, in law consent cannot be assumed and he was guilty of sexual exploitation of a child. This inevitably placed him too in the vulnerable prisoners' unit, which he resented bitterly. The authorities believed that Jones had become aware that Michael Ryan was to be transferred to another prison nearer to court where he was to face further charges of corruption. This presented an opportunity to plan an assault on York without the likelihood of the staff being informed in advance. So Jones had bided his time and chose his moment to be in the shower area at the same time as York. A distraction was arranged to draw staff away while he assisted York to slip heavily, bang his head on the floor and take several kicks to the body before help arrived and Jones could claim to have been assisting him. York had learnt enough about prison culture by that point to realise that it was not in his interests to accuse Jones and chose to maintain that he had slipped on his own.

Chapter Thirty

Rory was pleased to have met his cousin, and after her disclosures and more tears they parted in good heart, both not wanting to embark on any attempts at full-scale family integration but left the door open for any future questions that may emerge.

George Tiller, he contemplated. So that was a hugely significant part of the picture. It seemed that George was his real great-grandfather, not the drunken disgraced Sam Carpenter. That was a relief and brought warm feelings in its wake. From his discoveries so far, Rory was pleased to know that he came from solid hard-working English stock and that Sam Carpenter was a distraction. The question remained, however, what could he discover about George Tiller and what did actually happen around the time that he was said to have left for Australia? Rory also felt that there was another connection that he was missing, but couldn't quite figure it out. He set in motion another search of records in Australia in relation to the discovery of this new name.

Rory looked though his diary to identify the next opportunity to visit the library again and start to investigate the archives and newspaper reports for anything about George Tiller from around the turn of the twentieth century. He was keen to start to unfold the next chapter of his family history. Emma told him that he was getting obsessed with this and to chill out a bit, but Rory felt that after all this effort he had to see his enquiries through to a conclusion.

It was the following week that he made it to the library. Assisted by some information from various online sources, he was looking forward to comparing and validating what he had found. The picture that emerged about George Tiller was both fascinating and revealing. Newspaper reports, parish magazines and chronicles of the time described a man with a strong social conscience, a man embedded in the community, a man whom people looked up to and could trust. There were stories of his intervention with local landlords on behalf of the canal-travelling community when times were hard. Further stories included those of, securing church funds to help widows and orphans, early attempts at collective bargaining with the canal owners, organising community events and acting as a conciliator in local disputes between families. Rory felt increasingly proud of his great-grandfather and confident that some of his own values and aspirations were at least partly attributable to him. This was the sort of family that he felt intrinsically connected to. This accounted for his chosen career path and direction in life in contrast to the corporate identity of the family who had nurtured him. Rory felt proud, relieved and vindicated. It was at that point that the connection became clear in his mind, the element that he couldn't quite grasp; of course his real father was a Mr Carpenter, but his mother was a Miss Tiller, the same name.

* * *

After trying to absorb this latest revelation, Rory decided to ring his newly found cousin Mandy to seek further information. If his mother was a Miss Tiller, what if any was her connection to his great-grandfather George Tiller, he wondered? He paused before picking up the phone, wondering what sort of reaction he might receive and what he might learn?

The phone rang out. He tried again.

'Hello.'

'Mandy?'

'Yes, who's calling?'

'Mandy, it's Rory, we met the other day in Worcester.'

'Oh, yes, can I help you?' Mandy replied tentatively.

'I do hope so. Mandy, I'm trying to piece together in my mind a picture of the family over the generations. It occurs to me, given my parents' surnames, were they related at all?'

Mandy hesitated for a moment, trying to remember herself. 'Um... Rory, I'm just trying to remember... yes, yes of course. I remember being told that your mum was born in Canada, the daughter of our great-grandfather's second child. He was killed in the war. He had joined the Canadian forces and was killed on D Day on the beach landings. She then came back to England to go to university and that's where they met.'

'I see, how interesting, but why was she a Tiller and not a Carpenter, at least by name?' asked Rory.

'Rory, I think when our great-grandmother remarried Sam Carpenter, they changed the three children's name from Tiller to Carpenter, as people did then. Your grandfather, the fourth child was born a Carpenter, as you know, although we believe that he was conceived by George Tiller. Then I think your mum's father who was sent to Canada changed his own name back to Tiller.'

'That being out of regard for George and distain for Sam?' postulated Rory.

'Presumably,' Mandy replied.

'So my parents were actually cousins, although they wouldn't have known that until they met at university?' Rory enquired.

'Yes, that's right. In fact, given the fleeting nature of their relationship and what happened, I'm not sure that they would have known?'

* * *

Later, whilst walking Bracken along the canal towpath, Rory was feeling very pleased with himself about his progress in unravelling his family history. Bracken ran back and forth chasing sticks oblivious to his master's quest. Rory was heading for The Old Plough in the village where he had arranged to meet Joseph for a drink. He was excited about the prospect of sharing his discoveries with his friend and colleague. Bracken was familiar with the route too and ran ahead to the pub to find the dog drinking bowl and the prospect of any scraps left under the outside tables. He quickly emerged with the remnants of a bacon sandwich held proudly in his mouth. Rory tied his lead to the bench allowing him to polish off his quarry and went inside hoping to find Joseph. He was there looking comfortable sitting by the bar. The two men shook hands, ordered some drinks and went to sit outside.

'Cheers, Rory, you have good news to tell me I gather?' said Joseph warmly.

'Yes, I'm confident that I've traced my family history back to my great-grandfather who was something of a campaigner and social reformer!' replied Rory.

'Well done! Hey this beer really is good. Are you drinking your usual Iceberg?'

'Yes indeed,' Rory replied before telling Joseph all about his discoveries. Joseph was pleased for him and hoped that it would allow Rory to feel more at ease with himself. The two men chatted, enjoyed a few more beers and a good pub steak before setting off on their separate ways.

Chapter Thirty-One

Work was busy and Rory had to concentrate hard and discipline himself not to be distracted. All his cases deserved of his best and the process of prioritising and dividing his time was always challenging. He knew that he needed to keep up with developments in the York case. He was aware that York had been assaulted by his fellow prisoners but that the injuries were fairly minor. That's part of prison life I'm afraid, he thought. Also given Donald York's attitude when he visited him, Rory didn't consider that there was much that he could do at present. He concluded that he could wait to hear of any developments from the prison and keep in touch with Shaun and Becky about any news regarding further charges and their wider investigation.

Other work had to take priority. He set about writing several court reports that were soon to be required and must be completed on time. Late work was not an option. Rory enjoyed his job for the most part but wished that time wasn't always so tight and that resources weren't always so stretched. The team was busy enough but was also carrying two vacancies with no immediate prospect of appointing replacements.

A fraud case was also flagging up a need for intervention. A serious fraudster was due for release from a ten-year sentence in three months, and release arrangements needed to be confirmed. The man had set up a call centre to trawl phone records and target the elderly to ring them at home and con them. He ran several different approaches including telling his victims that they had won money on their Premium Bonds and asking for their bank details in order to pay them their winnings. Most recipients of such calls he found would readily believe him, disclose their bank details only to find out later that their account had been plundered not enhanced. Despicable, Rory thought. The offender wanted to be released to his own luxury flat in Burton but Rory was keen to see him resettle initially in probation hostel accommodation somewhere in the West Midlands to allow for greater oversight. A move back to Burton could then follow later, after say six months. Although probably not to his luxury flat, that was likely to be sold under 'proceeds of crime' provision. This involved powers to seize assets gained by crime that couldn't be traced to any rightful owners and to sell them and add the money to the public purse.

Chapter Thirty-Two

For the next stage in his journey of discovery Rory wanted to travel north along the Trent and Mersey canal, from Great Haywood. This would take him to Stone via Aston Marina, on to Stoke-on-Trent and then on to Leek in The Staffordshire Moorlands on the Caldon canal. So far as his research had revealed, this was one of the routes used regularly by his great-grandfather in transporting coal through The Potteries and taking china products back to the Midlands. He felt excited by the prospect of treading in his family's shoes. Could they also involve using some of the lock gates made by his forebears, he wondered?

Emma had agreed to join him again as long as he wasn't totally obsessed with chasing rainbows and agreed to talk about other things too. Rory had readily agreed in order to secure the company of his dear sister. They booked a date in late September for a six-day trip, this time feeling confident that they had calculated correctly to reach Leek and be able to turn round and return comfortably within the allotted time.

On the day of departure Rory arrived early at their prearranged meeting point at the boatyard, in order to load up their provisions. He bought some good fresh vegetables, bacon and sausages from the canal shop opposite and was pleased to have made most of the arrangements this time, taking the pressure off Emma. She had been working in Birmingham for the past few days so wasn't too far away. Nevertheless, he anticipated the last minute call announcing her late arrival at some point, given her frenetic lifestyle. In the event, Emma was only fifteen minutes late, having been delayed on the M6. She bounced across the yard, pecked him on the cheek and insisted that they set off immediately.

Emma confidently steered the boat out of the yard and headed north. She talked incessantly about her work. She wanted to share the details with Rory but also not to give him an opening to dominate the conversation with yet more family history revelations. Emma was pleased for him and hoped it would make him more content and less restless but didn't share his passion for the subject.

The late September weather was kind and a light breeze helped push them through the water and on towards Aston Marina for lunch. Their journey took them past the quintessential English villages of Weston and Salt, through Sandon lock with its smartly refurbished lock house and on past Burston. The strong connection between village life, the canals and the role of the country pub was evident. The journey was so peaceful and relaxing, strengthening Rory's sense of connection with the history of the canal network.

'I know you've done all the shopping, Rory, but are you sure you have everything?' she asked, reeling off a long list of requirements and hoping to take advantage of the fine foods available in the marina shop.

Rory just sighed and let her indulge. She came back with a full bag of shopping including food to make dinner later that evening. There goes the meal in the pub he thought, but smiled, happy to let her cook if she wanted to. Cooking was almost a novelty for Emma who spent much of her time on the road and living in hotels. Cooking in at least took the pressure of trying to identify somewhere to eat out and gave them more flexibility about where to moor up for the night. Rory set off walking with Bracken along the next stage whilst Emma continued to captain the ship. Had his family walked this very path, he thought? What stories may lie in these clods, what memories were locked in these hedgerows?

When Emma pulled in to navigate the next series of locks at Meaford, Rory operated the gates while Bracken struck up a tail-wagging contest with a Red Setter on the following boat. Once safely through the locks they both rejoined Emma on the boat.

'We could hire a bigger one next time and bring some friends along, what do you think, Emma?' asked Rory.

'No,' she said firmly. 'I like it with just the two of us,' and that was that.

As the afternoon drew on, they approached Barlaston and a suitable stopping point emerged just past the road bridge where there were a few shops. The road soon reached a level crossing. The railway track ran in close parallel to the canal, along the valley bottom. They pulled in, put out the camping chairs and sat down with a cup of Earl Grey. Bracken waited eagerly for any passers-by who he assumed were there for his benefit and would throw him a stick.

'My relatives could have moored up in this very spot, Em, don't you think?' Rory announced with excitement.

'Quite possibly, Rory, they may all emerge out of the water at any moment and join us for tea!' she replied as he pushed her playfully and she fell off her chair landing in a heap with Bracken on top of her licking her face furiously.

After spending a pleasant hour or so reading, they both set off to walk along the bank much to Bracken's delight. He bounded on ahead and off into a field on the left returning caked in mud and cowpats.

'Oh Bracken! Does he swim? He's not coming onboard the boat like that. He'll have to have a dip in the canal,' Emma pronounced as Rory tried to grapple with the slippery mess and steer him towards the canal. Bracken pulled him along, he lost his footing and unceremoniously the two of them slid down the bank and into the cold murky water. Fortunately, Rory was only wearing light clothing and had nothing of value in his pockets. Emma just stood on the side and laughed as her two bedraggled shipmates emerged from the cut. At least Bracken did look a little cleaner.

As Rory headed back to the boat to change, Emma carried on with Bracken towards the next bridge, number 104. 'Serves him right for pushing me over,' she thought aloud. 'No sympathy.' After a while she sat down on a fence while Bracken surveyed the area. He seemed particularly interested in one spot, in a little copse just left of the track by the bridge. It was there that he started digging. Initially, she took little notice but as he persisted, Emma joined him to see what was attracting such vigorous attention. As she looked over the fence at the site of his frantic digging the last thing that she expected to see was what looked very much like the bone structure of an outstretched human hand. Shocked, she took hold of Bracken and pulled him back then ordered him to go and fetch Rory. Relieved and somewhat surprised she watched as Bracken set off at full sprint to find his master.

Back at the boat Rory had managed to shower, soak his clothes and get dressed. As he came up onto the deck he was met by a flying barking dog obviously very keen to secure his attention. Bracken stopped short of the boat, continued barking and gesturing back up the towpath. Is Emma hurt? he wondered, as he quickly left the boat and followed Bracken up the path.

When he reached Emma he was surprised to see the worried look on her usual confident, self-assured face. As if unable to speak she glanced across at where Bracken had been digging and it was obvious to Rory too that Bracken had uncovered a human hand, protruding from the ground.

* * *

Rory was slow to react to the ringing sound in his pocket and only answered the call just in time. It was Laura, his manager.

'Rory, sorry to interrupt your break but there's something I need to share with you,' she said.

'Go on,' replied Rory, not knowing what to expect.

'Rory, it seems that Donald York has managed to orchestrate a media campaign seeking to cast doubt on his conviction and to press for his immediate release!'

'But that's not true, Laura, he was found guilty, the evidence was clear. He's not going to be released for many years, if ever,' replied Rory, feeling unnerved.

'I know. Don't worry, Rory, there's no prospect of immediate release. I just thought I had better let you know in case you heard or read some of the media coverage. There are other people in positions of power, not connected to this case who fear exposure, if this conviction encourages other historical victims of abuse to come forward. They are prepared to invest huge sums in trying to avoid that happening. York may feel that his friends have rallied round him, but in reality these people are only seeking to protect themselves. They want to discourage the media appetite to uncover more cases of people falling from grace. They seek to cast doubt in general on the very existence of child sexual abuse. If you do hear it on the news, don't be surprised that any official response is low key. Remember that the agreed approach is not to overreact to such stories.'

'Oh, I see, yes of course. Thank you, I'll bear that in mind,' he said feeling flustered.

Laura rang off sensing Rory's unease, wondering whether she had done the right thing by ringing him and why he was so agitated while on holiday? You can't win, she thought, but on balance felt that she was right to forewarn him.

* * *

It wasn't long before the police forensic team had the area taped off and a tent erected over the site of the discovery. It had taken some time to be put through to the right people, given that an emergency 999 response wasn't appropriate as there was no chance of saving a life in this case. Once connected to the right team, Rory had been impressed by their rapid response. He didn't know any of the officers concerned, but felt reassured that they would deal with this grisly discovery appropriately. Detailed statements were taken from him and Emma. He wondered whether they thought that they were responsible, then he satisfied himself that they needed to cover every angle. In essence, their statements were simple; that Bracken had found the body and he of course wasn't in a position to explain how or why. He was just doing what dogs do and being inquisitive.

The team set about carefully digging up the surrounding area. The earth was stable and had clearly not been disturbed for a long time. The recent wet weather, however, had allowed the hand to move closer to the surface and hence be discovered, the officer told them. After several hours of meticulous excavation, Rory and Emma were informed that they had managed to uncover a full human skeleton.

A little while later, one of the investigators approached Rory and explained that the body would be taken away for full forensic examination. Initial indications were that the skeleton was male and appeared to have suffered a substantial head injury. That was all that could be said at that point. The tent and taped-off area would remain for the time being and Rory and Emma were informed that they were free to carry on with their journey. The experience had been quite unnerving for both of them as they went back on board the boat. Emma was pleased that at least they were secure for the night. Dinner proved to be a subdued affair. It was a clear evening and they sat out on the towpath with a glass of wine after the officers had gone. Every passer-by bestowed them with official status and either sought an explanation for the police activity, permission to proceed or asked for any diversionary directions. After a while this got a little tedious and they retreated inside the boat.

'Poor man,' said Emma. 'I wonder who he was and what happened? Fancy being left there!' she exclaimed.

'It could be anyone. I wonder how long you have to be in the ground to become a skeleton? It could be someone reported missing?' responded Rory. He was surprised just how upset Emma was and sat holding her hand.

'Yes, some poor relative left not knowing and about to hear the worst. Sudden disappearance must be terribly difficult to deal with,' Emma speculated.

'Yes, I don't know how I'd feel in the circumstances. Being found here also seems odd, I don't know what to think?'

They continued to speculate and attempt to comfort each other. They considered whether it would be right to carry on their journey or simply return out of respect. After some thought they decided that these things happen, that it was a random find and that their actions either way would have no impact on the investigation and least of all the poor person and their family. Therefore they felt that they should carry on in the morning and try to put it behind them. Neither of them slept particularly well and even Bracken seemed to sense that something was wrong as he looked up at them and whined.

In the morning they quickly set off to leave the unpleasant scene behind them, travelling on towards Stoke. Their intention was to stop somewhere on the route towards Festival Park. This had been the site, Rory thought, of the first National Garden Exhibition and The Marina had been integral to the original design. They could get to the city or to Newcastle from there and find somewhere to eat. As if to add to their subdued mood it started to rain and the journey proved to be an unpleasantly wet experience. Emma laughed as she pointed out that Rory had already established a close connection with canal water and should be used to being wet by now! She sat inside and read her book while he stoically drove the boat north. They passed Hanford and Fenton and stopped as they approached Hanley before the turn onto the Caldon canal for the next leg of their journey towards Leek. They arrived too late to linger for tea and to set off immediately into the urban expanse of Stoke-on-Trent.

Rory was trying to explain to Emma the local history and geography but she found it all very confusing.

'So, Stoke-on-Trent city is actually Hanley, based on the five towns, although there are actually more than that, aren't they?' she asked.

'Yes that's right, there's actually seven towns; Hanley, Fenton, Burslem, Trentham, Longton, Tunstall and Stoke – all make up what is referred to as The Potteries and the city of Stoke-on-Trent.'

'What about Newcastle?' Emma asked.

'Well, Newcastle has always seen itself as separate apparently,' replied Rory, not entirely sure himself.

As they walked towards the city, they passed a bus stop at the right time and hopped onto a bus to get out of the rain. They toured through the streets of Hanley with its mixture of old and new and the ever present sense of its industrial past. They chose to alight in the centre and walked down the main street, window shopping. Emma wasn't familiar with this area and noted the contrast with Birmingham. She looked through the windows of various shops while Rory found a cash point. Opting not to find a pub they looked directly for an Indian restaurant and called in to sample a local curry. The Indian waiter had a strong Stoke accent and was very friendly. He took their order while they enjoyed some papadoms and a glass of Cobra. The main course proved to be excellent. Rory had ordered a chicken tikka rogan josh and Emma a prawn korma, which they shared with mushroom pilau rice and a garlic naan.

Afterwards they walked through the streets again for a while before concluding that they had better hire a taxi if they were to find their way back to the boat. They arrived back in good spirits after the traumatic events earlier in the day. The weather had cleared and they were able to stand outside on the back of the boat for a while before turning in for the night. Sleep inevitably was difficult after such an unusual and eventful couple of days.

The next morning Emma and Rory set off in better weather for Leek, a charming old-world town in the north of the county. Much of the route reflected its industrial heritage interspersed with the countryside beyond the city boundary. The route proved to be interesting with towns and villages, bridges and locks as they chugged on north-east towards Hazelhurst Junction, Leek Tunnel and the Aqueduct. Passing through the tunnel revived thoughts of those who worked the canals in times past, lying on their backs on their boats and stepping along the roof of the tunnel to propel the boat through. In those days, prior to the petrol engine, barges were horse drawn, hence the name – towpath.

* * *

After further enquiries Becky was able to confirm that money hived off from Auldbeck could be linked to an account of what was now a new project. She shared her findings with her DCI.

'Sir, I've checked this thoroughly. Money has been transferred through different accounts but I'm sure that there is a connection to a current local initiative…' she hesitated before mentioning its name: 'The Community Bridge Project.'

'Ah, I see,' replied Shaun not able to hide his discomfort. 'That's the scheme launched a few years ago as a local community partnership? One that's done well in helping disadvantaged young people to turn their lives around?'

'Yes, Sir.'

'Um, awkward isn't it? One to refer upstairs I think, Becky. Ironic isn't it, how things turn out sometimes?' he said rhetorically. 'Maybe it's time to let sleeping dogs lie with this one, but we'll let others agonise over that, Becky. I think you've done all you can on chasing this aspect of the case now.'

'OK, Sir,' replied Becky philosophically.

* * *

The canal weaved its way through the hills and into Leek, allowing for another overnight stay and the prospect of exploring places to eat in the town.

As they walked along, Rory was thinking how pleased he was to be with his sister, to share both the enjoyment of their holiday and the shock of discovering the body in the copse yesterday. Who was the poor person, he wondered? What were the circumstances of his or her death? All this, he thought, had been a distraction from his aim of creating time to reflect on his own circumstances, not of those of a complete stranger!

As they walked along, Emma took his arm and looked up at him: 'Rory, it's been so good to have you near this week.'

Nice though it was to hear, for Rory it just added to his sense of confusion. Their relationship had changed, entirely due to factors beyond their control and he was struggling with trying to make the adjustment.

'Do you fancy a pub meal, Rory?' Emma asked, still clinging to his arm.

'Actually yes, I was thinking that too. How about the Roebuck, the Titanic pub? I've not been to that one yet, but mates at work say it's worth a visit. The brewery took it over in 2011, apparently, and it's gone from strength to strength.'

'Yes, that sounds just great,' she replied. 'Rory, I can't stop thinking about the body –who was that person and why would someone be buried at the side of a canal? It doesn't make sense.'

The Roebuck proved to be a great success with the usual fine Titanic ales and a good selection of food to choose from. They enjoyed the experience and walked back to the boat feeling more relaxed. Tomorrow would herald the start of their return journey. Three days back along the same route. They had decided to vary all the stopping places and were looking forward to enjoying the trip from the opposite direction. Rory thought that it would also be a last chance this time to consolidate his thinking about not only his background and its implications for his identity, but also where that left him with his relationship with Emma?

* * *

Early into the return journey the following morning Rory took a call on his mobile. It was from the police. The forensic investigation had revealed that the body was in fact an adult male who had probably died from a head injury and dated from around the early part of the last century. So it was not a recent death or linked to any current missing person's investigation. The body also had an old injury to the left leg which was likely to have caused a substantial limp. However, the caller did not seem confident that the police investigation in those circumstances would be able to readily confirm the actual identity of the deceased.

'Isn't there DNA available?' Rory asked.

'Yes,' said the officer, 'we're waiting for the results now.'

Rory came off the phone and sat down.

'Are you OK, Rory, you look like you've just seen a ghost?' Emma asked.

'Maybe I have,' he replied. 'Emma, do you think it's possible that this skeleton belonged to someone who worked on the canals, someone who would have been around at the same time as my great-grandfather?'

'I suppose so,' replied Emma, sounding sceptical.

'Why would someone be buried there? Maybe in those days that was what canal people did? Maybe they didn't use churchyards?'

'Or that whoever buried him didn't want anyone else to know?' Emma responded.

'Why would that be?' asked Rory.

'Oh, Rory, for a probation officer you are terribly naive sometimes. If the man died from a head injury that doesn't sound like natural causes does it?'

'No, I suppose not. Do you think it suggests foul play?'

'I would say so, wouldn't you? It's certainly a possibility,' Emma replied.

* * *

By the time they approached Great Haywood, Emma and Rory had managed to enjoy the rest of their holiday without being too distracted by the events surrounding the discovery of the body. The experience of the return trip had, as they had expected, been interesting to view things from the opposite perspective. It also reinforced the view that as modern life continues to speed things up, something had been lost in taking your time; in having time to think.

Emma could tell that Rory was still troubled by his discoveries but felt confident that he would get over it. She also wondered where his thoughts would lead in relation to his future. As always, however, Emma felt pretty clear in her own mind where she was heading.

On reaching Great Haywood they handed the boat over, thanked the staff and went across the road for a drink in the cafe before heading off for home. They reaffirmed how good it felt to be able to spend more time together. Despite the interruption, it had still been worth it. Emma was due to be in London the following week and was not looking forward to the contrast in pace between chugging along the canal and life back in the fast lane. Rory was trying not to think what would be waiting for him on his return to work. The ease of modern communication ensured a mass of messages for anyone who had dared to leave their desk and precious computer for more than a few hours, let alone a week! He'd deal with that tomorrow. After a hug and exchange of best wishes Rory waved Emma goodbye, with a note of sadness before securing Bracken in the car and heading for home.

In an attempt not to start thinking about work, Rory retrieved his file about his family research. On reading through his notes again he discovered a reference to his

139

great-grandfather having had a serious accident at work as a young man, involving a fall into an empty canal lock which had left him with a permanent limp. As he read on, his source had definitely stated that the limp was in relation to his left leg.

Rory froze for a moment. This could be just chance, or was it, he thought?

Could this be? Was it possible? Could this body actually be his great-grandfather who had supposedly emigrated to Australia and for whom no records could be found of his arrival; the body of a man who worked the canals and spent much of his life in the area where the discovery was made? Could he have sustained another injury at work, or was it something else, as Emma had suggested? Rory immediately rang the police. He felt that he must let the forensic team know. The officer he spoke to took note of his observations. Within the hour he received a call back, the DNA results had been delivered back to the police. The officer asked if they could check the body's DNA against his own in the light of his observation. Rory readily consented. He suggested that his natural mother, Miss Tiller, may provide further confirmation if her DNA was on file somewhere?

Whilst at work several days later, Rory took a further call confirming a close match between the DNA samples strongly suggesting that the body that Bracken had uncovered on the canal towpath was in fact his great-grandfather George Tiller. But he was not expecting the further disclosure. The officer was able to tell him that the search on the DNA database also revealed another match.

'A match with whom?' he asked.

'Molly Bennett, Sir,' he replied.

Chapter Thirty-Three

Rory wanted to immediately embark on unravelling this new line of enquiry, trying to throw light on the connection with Molly Bennett. Different thoughts rushed through his head. How might he be connected to Molly Bennett and where would that leave him with the York case? He mentioned it to Laura, his manager, as it would not be appropriate for him to continue to supervise Donald York's case if this connection proved to be real.

At his next available opportunity, Rory tried to look into the connection in more detail. With the help of parish records, the census and cooperation from the police, it seemed that Molly Bennett was probably the illegitimate daughter of his grandfather; the same status that belonged to his grandfather's first son. Further investigation and consultation revealed that after getting married, his grandfather went on to have five more children. As was common practice at the time in large extended families, it seemed that he had simply given his two illegitimate children to relatives who were unable to have their own. This was an arrangement entirely within the family with no official involvement and none was deemed necessary. The two children then reappeared on official records later. They had subsequently moved away with their new family who left to seek employment elsewhere on the railways. It was only when their new parents both died in a train accident at work that they were taken into care and eventually had the misfortune to arrive at Auldbeck.

Rory was nearing the end of his quest for family information but the one remaining part of the story that he was yet to discover was what exactly had led to the death of George Tiller. After months of chasing, Rory was at the point of giving up when Shaun rang him and said as a result of a casual conversation with an old police mate he had learnt of the existence of a small private museum of constabulary in Burton in the south-east of the county. He understood that the museum had an extensive collection of old police pocket books from the 1890s onwards and may have some information about George Tiller.

Rory was due to go to Burton later that week to discuss the handover of a complex case and to affect a transfer. He arranged to visit the museum after work with the kind cooperation of the curator. On the day, Rory already felt drained but knew that he couldn't ease up now. He drove through the town and the busy rush hour traffic to find the small understated museum. The lady curator was lovely, warm-hearted and so kind as she ushered him inside. For her, this was obviously a labour of love. She explained the history of the project while making some tea and even produced some freshly baked scones. Rory was impressed and grateful as he realised that he hadn't had time for any lunch, so the scones were very welcome. She led him through the two front rooms of what was a traditional terraced house now lined with helmets, handcuffs and truncheons. Old photographs of royal visits, promotions and civic affairs hung on the walls as if guarding the establishment. They continued into the back kitchen. From there a narrow staircase led down to a cellar. Past cobwebs and dust down into the bowels of the house lay hundreds of small boxes, each carefully labelled and piled in some kind of order known only to the lady herself.

She paused for a moment and pointed him in the direction of a stack of several boxes in the corner saying, 'That may be what you are looking for; my collection of local police pocket books from 1916. Sometimes the years overlap so you might have to check 1915 and 1917 too but I suggest that you start there with 1916. I'll leave you to it.'

The light was poor as Rory started what he felt could be a Herculean task. He opened the first box and found the books all neatly placed in rows and filed alphabetically according to the name of the officer. Most were PCs, often village bobbies. Notes included entries on scrumping, bunking off school, minor shoplifting, drunkenness and vagrancy, but nothing as serious as murder. How could he possibly sift through all these, he thought? He was sure that he didn't know the name of the local constable from that time in the area where the skeleton was found. Then on closer inspection, not all the boxes were filed in the same way. At the bottom of the stack were three boxes that claimed to contain pocket books relating to the war, agricultural matters and finally canals. With a growing sense of excitement Rory set about trawling through the canal box.

After several hours, Rory came across the notebook of one PC Alfred Fletcher, the police officer responsible for the canal, written in the summer of 1916. It contained detailed accounts of various incidents between bargees and local people. The first account he read related to an accusation of theft of bacon from the butcher whilst he cycled along the canal towpath. It claimed that the butcher was deliberately distracted by one man whilst his brother took the bacon from the basket on the front of his bike. Rory read on and flicked through several more pages until there it was, an account of an altercation between George Tiller, a bargee and William Stock an agent representing the canal owners. A Tilly Fairweather had reported to the constable that she had heard shouting and an angry exchange between the two men on the night of 1st July. William Stock had come to tell George that he was to reduce his team further from five down to three men and that the owner still expected him to run two boats and carry the same amount of goods. The other two men had volunteered for the army as had two workers before them. George had claimed that this would be impossible but Stock simply told him to do it or volunteer himself, if he was man enough. George took exception to the insult, claiming that unlike him, Stock had bought his medical exception from military service and at that Stock had struck him down with a lock gate handle and left him bleeding on the towpath. Tilly had not thought anything of it at the time but by the morning the blood had been cleared up and George was never seen again, and it was later said that he had left for the new world.

So there it was, a contemporary account of what had happened. The implication was clear that William Stock had killed his great-grandfather, buried him near the towpath and put about the story of his emigration. It was also likely that police resources would have been severely stretched at that time due to the war and there was no enthusiasm to investigate this incident any further. It was simply put down to an argument between two local men when blows were exchanged. In other words that it was nothing unusual. Rory knew that he could never prove it but felt satisfied that he had found what had really happened. As George's wife had maintained, it was totally out of character for him to just up sticks and leave all that was dear to him. She was right, he hadn't left at all but had died that night and remained undiscovered for a hundred years until the dog of his great-grandson happened to sense his presence in the ground. At last George could be laid to rest properly. With the kind cooperation of the museum curator, Rory was able to borrow his find and left with the pocketbook to be able to show Emma. He so wanted her to see it for herself.

He left, feeling a flood of emotions, of confusion mixed with satisfaction, of some pleasure at reaching a conclusion, but with unease about the outcome. There was also the prospect of a funeral to come. How odd to be faced with potentially burying a man who had died a hundred years ago, he pondered. Still, other things were becoming clearer in his mind.

At the next opportunity the following weekend, he showed Emma the book and described his search at the museum to her in detail. Emma, who had not been particularly impressed by his stoic efforts so far, began to cry. She had tried so hard to stay strong for him, to keep him grounded, but this discovery had really touched her heart.

'The poor dear,' she said, 'and poor you too,' with tears

rolling down her cheeks.

'Oh, sis, thank you,' he replied, touching her arm, 'but I'm so pleased to have found an answer. I'll leave it now, it's done Now I know who I am.'

After a pause for Rory to offer the comfort of a large handkerchief, Emma looked up at him and said, 'Rory, you really must stop calling me that now,' as she stemmed her tears.

'Oh yes you're right,' he said and took a deep breath. 'Now that it's finally clear that you aren't really my sister – Emma, will you marry me?' asked Rory expectantly.

'Yes, Rory, of course,' she replied, as the tears returned.

Lightning Source UK Ltd.
Milton Keynes UK
UKHW010744131219
355185UK00002B/45/P

9 781787 193864